Standalone

Love Me or Hate Me

Campus Games Series

THE FINAL GAME

CAMPUS GAMES BOOK #4.5

STEPHANIE ALVES

Editing: AVA Book Editing

Cover designer: Stephanie Alves

Characters: Nmvector

ISBN: 978-1-917180-11-5

This book contains detailed sexual content, graphic language and some other heavy topics.

You can see the full list of content warnings on my website here: stephaniealvesauthor.com

Happy Reading!

To everyone who finds comfort in found family and wants love that's given freely, not just because it's expected.

The Proposal

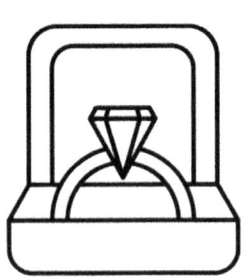

Chapter 1

"I'm getting married!"

My balls shrivel at the high-pitched sound of Gabi's voice outside our hotel room.

"Get the fuck out of here," I yell back, groaning when I roll off my girlfriend at the feeling of my dick slip out of her.

"Put your dick away," Gabi shouts from the other side of the door. "This is ten times more important. I'm getting married."

"We know," Rosie and I say in unison. My angel laughs, snuggling her head into the crook of my neck.

Gabi hasn't stopped yelling to the world that in three days, she'll be married to Chris.

Honestly, I wasn't too irritated by it when she got engaged. She was happy. I got that. But since then, it hasn't stopped. For over a year, she has been constantly reminding everyone that she's going to get married.

Every. Single. Day.

My eyes narrow down at Rosie, who bites her bottom lip to stifle a laugh. "Whose brilliant idea was it to book a hotel room right next to Gabi's?" I ask with a huff.

She lifts her head, her lips curling into a gorgeous smile. "Come on, she's happy," my beautiful girlfriend tells me. She's too good for this world, too good for me. I'll never stop thanking the universe for bringing her into my life. "Besides, it's been so long since we've all been together."

"And that's a good thing," I reply with a smirk, wrapping my arm around her waist to pull her closer to me. "If we had booked any other room, I'd be inside of you right now." Her breaths become labored when I press my lips to the hollow of her neck, breathing in her sweet, fresh scent. "I'd be buried deep inside your pussy, fucking you until you came all over my cock."

"Grayson," she whispers, the sound hushed as she tips her head back, and widens her legs, making room for me.

"*God*, angel. I fucking love you." I settle myself on top of her, ready to slide home when another three annoying knocks hit the hotel room door.

I squeeze my eyes shut and let out a groan, kicking off the sheets. "I'm going to fucking kill her." I quickly pull myself out of bed, throw on my boxers, and open the door to the biggest cockblock of the century. "What the fuck do you want?"

Gabi's face twists when she sees me at the door, and she dramatically slaps her hands over her eyes. "Ew. Put that away."

"I'm wearing boxers," I drawl.

"And it's fucking gross," she replies with a groan. "The only dick I want to see is my husband's."

I press my lips together, amusement rolling through me. "My dick's away, and Chris isn't your husband *yet*."

She spreads her fingers, cracking an eye open between them. "He'll be my husband soon."

2

I tilt my head. "Then I guess that means you can't see his dick until tomorrow, then."

She drops her hands, narrowing her blue eyes at me. "I hate when you're logical and shit. Go back to being dumb," she says with a wave of her hand.

My brows dip, and I let out a scoff. "I was never dumb."

"You were when you ended things with Rosie because you were scared of *love*," she mocks, rolling her eyes.

"You're still talking about that?" I ask with a shake of my head. "That happened nine years ago."

She lifts her shoulder in a shrug. "I don't forgive and forget."

I shake my head, running a hand through my hair. Gabi can hold a grudge like no one else. I'd be sorry for Chris if I didn't know those two were made for each other. They share one mind, one body, one soul. Even clothes sometimes. It's weird.

Actually, it's kind of cute. I'd never admit that to her though.

She might not forgive me for breaking Rosie's heart all those years ago, but maybe she will if she knows what I'm planning.

Am I really going to do this? Am I really going to tell the one person who can't keep a secret to save her life *my* biggest secret?

Fuck it. I lean forward, gently closing the door behind me, so Rosie doesn't hear. "What if I tell you I'm going to ask her to marry me?" I whisper.

3

Gabi's jaw drops and her eyes widen so much I almost think they're going to pop out of her head. "What?" she yells.

"The point of whispering is to not make a scene," I whisper-hiss at her, closing my eyes with a groan. "I knew I shouldn't have told you."

"No. No. No," she repeats, shaking her head. "I can keep it a secret. I won't tell anyone, I promise."

"You sure?" I ask, skeptically, raising a brow at her.

"Yes," she replies with a roll of her eyes. "I know how to keep a secret."

"I highly doubt that."

Her eyes narrow when I let out a scoff. "You don't know what I know. I might have the biggest secret of all, and you wouldn't even suspect a thing."

"Right," I say with a laugh.

Her face screws up and she shakes her head. "If only you…" She groans. "Never mind. It's not even worth it. Am I the only one who knows you're proposing?"

"Yeah," I admit with a smirk. "I was going to tell Aiden today."

"Wait." Her brows shoot up into her hairline. "I'm the first person you've told?"

"God help me," I breathe out, harshly, regretting all my decisions, "but yes."

"Oh my god!" Her squeal makes me wince, and I pray Rosie doesn't hear her. "I'm so excited."

"I can tell," I drawl, shaking my head. This might be the worst mistake I've ever made. "Are you sure you can keep this to yourself for a while?"

"Yes," she repeats with an eye roll. "Aside from Chris, I won't tell anyone."

My brow arches. "You're telling Chris?" I ask. "What happened to 'I won't tell anyone'?"

"Chris doesn't count," Gabi says with a scoff. "I tell him everything."

"Of course you do," I say, breathing out a laugh. I don't know why I'm surprised. Those two are attached at the hip. Besides, I'm planning on telling the guys at some point anyway.

"So, when are you going to ask her?" she asks, grinning like an idiot. But then her smile drops, and she pins me with a murderous glare. "You're not going to ask her this weekend, right? Grayson Carter Livingston, I swear to all that is holy in this world, if you steal my thunder—"

"Calm down." I raise my hands defensively as she advances, her fist inches from my face. "I'm not going to steal your thunder."

She drops her hands, her face softening to something less murdery. "You're not?"

"No," I confirm, blowing out a breath. "But it'll be soon. I already have it all planned out and even stalked her laptop to find her dream ring," I admit.

Gabi's face lifts into a genuine smile, and she actually looks happy for me. "Finally," she breathes out a sigh, shaking her head. "Who would have thought you guys would be the last to get married?"

Yeah, I know. Nine years ago, I didn't even believe in love. But now, one look at the girl inside this room and I know

5

she's the love of my life. I knew in my heart I wanted to marry her years ago, but with her career taking off and her being so busy, I didn't want to take away any of her achievements.

From the very first moment I laid eyes on her at that frat party sophomore year, she's been mine. And she's been mine ever since. Even without a ring.

But I can't fucking wait to slip a ring on her finger, see her wear it every day, and watch her walk down the aisle in a gorgeous white dress, and be my wife.

My wife.

Fuck.

I want that. So. Bad.

"You're daydreaming, lover boy."

I snap out of my thoughts and shoot a glare at Gabi. She really does love interrupting all my fantasies, doesn't she?

"What are you doing here so early anyway? Your wedding is in three days, as you keep reminding us, not today."

"We're going for brunch," she says.

"We?"

A scoff leaves her lips. "Not you, obviously."

"Thanks," I say dryly.

"I mean the girls," she clarifies, with a shrug. "I need a day with my girls before the bachelorette party tomorrow."

"Right." I run a hand through my hair, nerves wracking through me at the thought of what the fuck is going to go down at Gabi's bachelorette party. Leila and Madi's were pretty tame, but this is Gabi we're talking about. "About that."

"Relax," she says, reading my expression. "We're just going to a bar. There will be drinks, dancing, you know," she says, lifting her shoulder in a shrug, "normal stuff."

"And who's going to be dancing?" I ask. If there's going to be strippers there, I might lose my shit.

"Ah. Ah. Ah," Gabi says, shaking her head with a tut. "Girls only. You don't get to know what we're doing."

I blow out a breath, deciding to keep my calm. This is her wedding after all. "Fine, just make sure Rosie's home early. I can't sleep without her," I admit.

Gabi scrunches her nose. "That's actually kind of cute," she says. "And don't worry, we won't stay out too late. I need my beauty sleep. I'm getting married this weekend."

"I know," I repeat with a groan for the umpteenth time.

"We all know!" Gabi and I turn our heads to see an older lady wearing a white robe while she pops her head out of the door, shooting a glare at Gabi. "It's all we've been hearing for the past two days."

When she slams the door closed, I press my lips together to stop my smile and glance at Gabi who has a scowl on her face. "Bite me," she mutters to the door.

A laugh leaves my lips as I reach over and knock on Gabi's door. "Chris, come get your wife. She's causing trouble again."

"Wife," Gabi murmurs to herself, a wide grin spreading across her face. "I love the sound of that."

I turn around so she doesn't see my smile and enter my room, closing the door behind me. I'm really happy for those two, even if Gabi does give me a headache sometimes.

7

"You're back." I lift my head, seeing Rosie walk out of the shower, a towel wrapped around her hot as fuck body, and her sunshine blonde hair tied up in a messy bun on the top of her head.

"Yeah," I reply, giving the most beautiful girl in the world a smile that's only reserved for her. "I'm back."

"What did Gabi want?" she asks, heading towards the counter to pick up her lotion, pumping some before spreading it across her smooth body.

"Apparently, she's taking you guys to brunch or something," I tell Rosie, walking up behind her and pressing my lips against her shoulder. Her skin is warm and so fucking soft, I want to drag her back to bed right now. "I bet she's going to spend the whole time talking your ear off about her wedding."

Rosie lets out a sweet little laugh, the sound like a drug injected into my veins. Her eyes light up, and she looks up at me with that radiant smile that never fails to make my heart race. "Give her a break. She's marrying the love of her life."

"Yeah," I agree, my gaze shifting to her reflection in the mirror. The sight of her takes my breath away, and I swallow hard as emotions clog my throat.

The thought of spending the rest of my life with the girl of my dreams fill my mind, and my heart races as our eyes meet in the mirror.

I can't wait to marry the love of *my* life.

Chapter 2

Our heads lift at the sound of Gabi groaning loudly as she devours her French toast.

"Are you having fun over there?" Leila asks with a chuckle, amused at the noises she's making. "If I didn't know any better, I'd assume you were pregnant or something by the way you're looking at that French toast." She gestures to her own round belly, and sighs. "Trust me, I would know."

"I'm amazing," Gabi slurs with a mouthful of French toast. "I'm incredible. I'm fucking fantastic." She shakes her head. "How did I not know how good French toast is?" she asks, groaning again. "I'm going to have to ask Chris to make these every day instead of pancakes from now on."

"Kinda feel bad for the guy," Madeline says, letting out a laugh as she glances at Gabi.

Leila lets out a scoff. "You're acting as if the guy wouldn't build a bakery if she wanted," she replies.

Gabi swallows down her food, before reaching for her orange juice, not mimosa—shocking I know—and takes a sip before a grin spreads across her face. "I love hearing you guys talk about my soon to be husband," she says, before taking another bite of her food.

"Are you excited?" I ask her, picking up some scrambled eggs on my fork before I swallow them down. "About finally being Mrs. Hudson?"

"I think she's more excited about the French toast right now," Madi pipes in with a chuckle.

"I wouldn't be so sure," Leila replies, sipping on her lemon water. "She's practically jumping out of her chair."

"It's the sugar," Madi replies with a chuckle as she glances at Gabi who's bouncing in her seat. "She's like a kid, I swear. Too much sugar and she's jumping off the walls."

Gabi chuckles, swallowing her food before she winks at us, holding up her orange juice. "I'll be jumping on other things later," she says with a mischievous grin.

Madeline sighs, a smile curving her lips. "Our best friend, ladies and gentlemen," she says, raising her glass as she arches a brow at Gabi. "Never change." Tipping her glass back, she swallows a sip of her mimosa.

"I never will," Gabi replies, taking a sip of her drink.

"Hmmm." Leila presses her lips together in a hum. "Not all change is bad," she says, pointedly. "Especially for the bachelorette tomorrow night."

Gabi lets out a loud gasp, placing a hand dramatically on her chest. "You want me to *change*?"

A laugh bubbles out of me as Leila rolls her eyes. "I don't mean to dye your hair and quit dancing. I just meant you may want to remember you're getting married this weekend, so getting trashed probably won't be the best decision."

"You don't have to worry," she reassures us with a wave of her hand. "I won't get trashed."

"Are you sure about that?" I ask with a chuckle. I've known Gabi for a long time, and knowing her means knowing she loves a good party, as much as she loves to get absolutely wasted.

"I'm very sure," she says with a grin as she picks up her orange juice. "I can promise you guys I'll be on my best behavior, and will be perfectly fine for the wedding."

Leila lets out a groan, dropping her hand to her belly. "I think the baby had too many croissants."

"How much longer until you're screaming in pain?" Gabi asks.

Leila pins her with a glare. "Not a huge fan of the way you put it," she says. "But there's still three weeks left." She lets out a sigh. "I can't wait to meet him."

Gabi freezes, her eyes widening. "Wait, it's a boy? I have a bet going with the guys that it's going to be a girl. Don't tell me I just lost."

Leila rolls her eyes. "Yeah, I know about that bet. But no, we don't know yet. Aiden wanted it to be a surprise this time, but I kind of think it's a boy," she admits, with a smile.

"I don't think it's going to be a boy," Madi pipes in, shaking her head. "Aiden screams 'girl dad'."

This whole talk of weddings and babies has my head spinning, and I tug on my bottom lip with my teeth, feeling every emotion under the sun. I've kept it bottled inside the whole morning, and I can't wait a second longer.

"I found a ring," I blurt out, letting out a heavy sigh once I finally let it out. My shoulders drop as the girls turn to face me, their jaws dropped.

"A… a ring?" Madeline asks, furrowing her brows.

"Like a cock ring?" Gabi asks, with an arched brow.

"Obviously she didn't mean that," Leila says dryly, turning her attention back to me. "You found an engagement ring?"

"It could still be a cock ring," Gabi pipes in with a shrug.

I press my lips together, and shake my head. "No. It's not… that," I affirm, feeling my cheeks heat up. "When Gabi knocked on our door and um… interrupted us," I begin, seeing Gabi smirk. "I was getting ready to take a shower, and I saw a small, black box in the drawer when I was trying to find my hairbrush. I wasn't going to open it but… it was right there, and I could tell it was a ring box, and so I opened it," I say, letting out a breath. "It was an engagement ring. A three-carat, oval diamond, excellent cut, D color, VS1 clarity engagement ring."

Madi's brows shoot up. "That's…"

"The exact one I want," I confirm with a nod. "Down to the gold band, encrusted with smaller diamonds."

"Wow," she says, surprised etched on her features. "How did Grayson know that's the one you wanted?" she asks.

I shake my head, a smile curling my lips. "I don't remember telling him what ring I wanted, and even if I did let it slip, I don't see how Grayson would have remem—"

"He said he saw it saved on your laptop," Gabi chimes in, her eyes fixed on her French toast as she takes another bite.

I blink down at her. "He… what?" I ask, my heart thumping in my chest.

She lifts her head, and her eyes widen as soon as she sees my expression, and presses her lips together. "I mean… Grayson's going to propose? *Whaaaat?* That's crazy. Brand new information. I had nooo idea."

12

I can't help but laugh at her poor attempt and pin her with a confused look. "You're really bad at lying," I say with a shake of my head.

Her lips part on a sigh and she slumps into her seat. "Fuck. I told him I could keep it a secret until he had the balls to propose."

"Oh my god," Leila says, swallowing hard as she locks eyes with me. "Grayson's really going to propose?"

"I guess so," I reply, my belly heating up, swarming with butterflies, feeling like the first time I ever kissed him. I still remember that day vividly. I still remember his smile, and his hands on me, and the noises he made.

It was the start of everything between us, and nine years later we're here, and he's going to propose. "Grayson is going to propose," I murmur to myself, still dumbfounded that this is really going to happen.

I've wanted to marry Grayson for years now. He makes me so happy, and I can't imagine my life without him. But being the CEO of my own fashion company has kept me busy, so I put the idea of marriage on the backburner. Our life was hectic and we didn't really have time, but I'd be lying if I said I wasn't a little disappointed that he never asked me to marry him. But now he's about to.

"How the hell did you know Grayson's going to propose?" Leila asks Gabi.

"He told me this morning," she admits, her gaze sliding to me. "I'm almost shocked you didn't hear my scream when I found out."

"I heard that," Madeline chimes in with an arched brow. "I thought it was a child."

"Close," Leila adds with a chuckle. "So… how are you feeling about this?" she asks, turning her green eyes on me.

"I'm good," I confirm with a happy sigh, my cheeks aching from smiling. "I'm really good. I'm so ready to be his wife."

"It's about time he popped the question, don't you think?" Madi lets out a laugh. "I mean, you guys were the first to get together, and the last to get married."

I shake my head, a smile spreading across my face. "I love him so much. I would have waited a lifetime for him."

Gabi drops her fork, and her face fills with an uneasy look and before we know it, she runs toward the bathroom.

"Who would have thought?" Leila says with a chuckle. "You actually made Gabi throw up with your talk of being in love."

"Got to give it to her, she really committed to the bit." Madi raises her glass and cheers with Leila. "Sometimes I think she might be a better actress than me."

"Hell no," Leila says with a scoff. "She's dramatic, for sure, and loves to cause a scene, and be the center of attention."

"Is there a but coming or…"

Leila smirks. "But she doesn't have three amazing movies and two TV shows under her belt like you do."

Madi smiles, tilting her head at Leila. "Fine. I'll give it to you. That *is* true."

I turn my head when I see Gabi back in her seat, reaching for a glass of water instead of the orange juice as she takes a sip. "Back already?" I ask her. "I kind of thought you'd stick to the bit a little longer," I say with a chuckle. "Did you really need to make a scene just because I said I loved Grayson?"

Gabi's lips twitch into a smile and she shrugs. "Couldn't help it," she says. "Love makes me barf."

Madi scoffs, shaking her head. "I can't wait to see how lovey-dovey you and Chris get at the wedding."

"That's different," Gabi says with a grin. "That's about me."

"Thanks," I say dryly, knowing she's joking.

A laugh bubbles out of her, but it settles when she meets my eyes. "I really am happy for you, Rosie. I can see how happy he makes you and how much you two love each other." My eyes start to tear up. "And I can't wait to be the maid of honor at your wedding."

"Excuse me?" Leila asks with narrowed eyes. "If anyone's going to be maid of honor, it'll be me."

"I'm the first who knew about the engagement," Gabi replies.

"And I was her best friend first."

A scoff leaves Gabi's lips. "You'll probably be pregnant again by the time she gets married. You won't have time to do everything a maid of honor needs to do."

"Guys," I interject with a laugh. "I love how passionate you guys are about being my maid of honor, but nothing's happened yet."

15

"I can be your maid of honor," Madi whispers, flashing me a smile. "I'm organized, planned an amazing wedding for Leila in just under three months, and I won't get drunk at the bachelorette party."

I chuckle, bringing the drink to my lips.

Nine years ago, I was lost and lonely and didn't know how my life would turn out.

And now I have these three amazing people, plus an amazing boyfriend who I can't wait to marry.

I just need to wait for him to propose first.

Chapter 3

"Anyone else want a drink?" James asks us, gesturing to the waitress holding a tray with four beers.

I shake my head. "I'm good," I tell him, lifting my half empty glass of beer. "Still working on this one."

Aiden arches a brow when his gaze slides to him. "Still don't drink," he says.

"I'll take one," Chris says, reaching for the glass before he takes a sip.

"No one else wants one?" James asks, looking around the booth before he lifts his shoulder in a shrug. "No? That's fine. More for me," he says, grabbing the three beers and positioning them in front of him.

I let out a laugh, shaking my head. "Are you ready to deal with puke tonight?" I ask James' husband, Carter, watching James start to gulp down his first beer.

Carter sighs, running a hand through his hair. "I'm used to it," he says with a smirk as he looks at his husband lovingly.

From the corner of my eye, I spot the waitress smiling down at Aiden, and I turn my head to see her lean down, the neckline of her T-shirt low as her cleavage spills out and she places a beer in front of him, along with a slip of paper that she slides beside the glass. "This one's on me," she says with a smile.

Aiden's eyes drop to the drink in front of him when she stands up straight and walks away, and he lifts his head to look at us. "Did she not hear me say I didn't drink?"

"I don't think the drink is what she wanted to give you," James points out with a chuckle, glancing down at the slip of paper on the table.

Aiden lets out a sigh, and picks up the piece of paper, ripping it up before he even reads it and throws the rips into the cigarette bowl in the middle of the table.

"Does that happen a lot?" I ask him, slightly amused at the scene. Aiden was a ladies' man in college, and I saw first-hand how girls threw themselves at him, but now… it's ten times worse. Being in the NBA was his dream for so long, and he finally made it, but with the fame comes millions of girls wanting in his pants. I've only gotten a little glimpse at what it's like to be him, and I genuinely feel sorry for the guy.

Sure, most guys wouldn't consider having girls want to sleep with them a curse, but for someone like Aiden, who's married to the love of his life, and is about to have a second child with her, it's the last thing he wants.

"All the fucking time," he replies with a sigh as he picks up his coke, taking a sip. "I'm sick of having to turn them down politely when all I want to do is lift my hand and show them my fucking ring."

"It really happens that much?" James asks, his brows shooting up to his hairline.

Aiden nods, his jaw clenching. "It really fucking kills me to think my wife is in our home worrying about some girl trying to get her hands on me." His face drops into a frown.

"She knows she's the love of my fucking life, and is so much more confident in knowing she's the only girl I'll ever want, but I know it's still hard for her, especially when I'm on the road."

We're all quiet for a bit, realizing how hard it must be for him to be away from Nova and Leila so much, since they haven't been to the away games while Leila's been pregnant."

"Jesus," James blurts out. "The mood has gone all the way down. You guys want to hear a fun story?"

Chris lets out a laugh. "All of your stories are about what you do in the bedroom," he says. "I think it's best to leave that between you and your husband."

James sighs, turning his attention to Carter. "They're so boring, aren't they, baby?" he jokes.

Carter shakes his head, attempting to scowl at him, but his lips turn into a smile. "You tell them way too much about our sex life," he replies with a laugh.

He's always been a reserved guy ever since I met him, but I don't think he minds the attention when it comes to James.

"I'm the exact same," Aiden says with a grin. "Leila hates it, and you guys know how much I love to annoy her."

I scoff. "You two are children," I say, gesturing to Aiden and Carter with my glass.

"We *have* children," Aiden corrects with a smirk.

"We?" James interrupts with wide eyes.

Those two made it clear they weren't going to have any children of their own, but that doesn't mean they don't love hounding us about having children so they can be their 'cool uncles'.

Aiden laughs. "Only me," he corrects, shaking his head when he sees James visibly relax. "And it's fucking amazing," he says with a huge smile. I thought the only person who could make him smile like that was Leila, but then came Nova and she stole Aiden's heart. And I have no doubt that this next one will be the same.

"It's time you caught up with me," he says, tilting his head at me. "And you guys, too." He lifts his chin at Lucas and Chris.

Lucas presses his lips together. "Just because you popped a baby in your wife less than two months after you guys were married, doesn't mean we're all the same."

Aiden makes a noise of agreements, sliding his gaze to me. "And when are you two going to have kids?" he asks. "Chris is marrying Gabi in two days, which means they'll be next."

"We will?" Chris says with a nervous laugh. I know full well that the guy wants a baby with Gabi, though. He's made it clear time and time again that he'd give her anything she wants no matter what.

Aiden smirks at him before turning his attention back to me. "Isn't it about time?" he asks.

I take a sip of my drink. I can't say I've dreamed of having kids, at least not before Rosie showed up in my life. Growing up with the father I had kind of soured me on the whole subject, but my biological dad was the best man I knew, and thinking about how he raised me, and how much I loved him… I think I'd make a pretty great dad.

I know for a fact Rosie would be an amazing mom. That girl is full of life, and smiles, and love, and always sees the

20

best in the world. And I can't pretend that the idea of seeing a little kid look like both Rosie and me doesn't make me smile.

Yeah, I think I might want kids after all.

"It's coming," I tell him, swallowing down my sip. "I have some other things I need to worry about first."

His brows bunch together. "Like what?" he asks. "I thought you guys were settling down in New York now."

"We are," I affirm with a nod. "That's not what I was talking about."

"Then what else is there?"

A grin pulls at my lips as I reach for the small, black box in my pocket and pull it out, opening it up to the guys.

Aiden freezes mid sip, and swallows harshly, placing the cup on the table. "Yes!" he says, fanning his face in a dramatic gesture that makes me roll my eyes. "Yes. Yes. A million times yes."

"You're a fucking idiot," I say with a scoff. "Shut the fuck up before you make a scene and this shit gets on the news before I can actually propose."

He lets out a laugh, his eyes zoning in on the ring. "Holy shit. You're really going to propose?" he asks.

"That's the plan," I tell the guys, my neck cracking at the thought. I'm so fucking excited for this next step, but I can't help the rush of nerves that flood through my body. What if she somehow says no? What if she doesn't want to marry me?

In the back of my mind I know it's a stupid idea, and that we're made for each other, but I can't help but think I'll never be good enough for her, even after nine years of being together.

Rosie is an angel. She's so sweet, and soft and kind, and fuck… I love her so much.

I just hope she wants to marry me as much as I want to marry her.

"What do you guys think?" I ask them, showing them the ring.

"It's beautiful," James says, his eyes widening at the ring. "It must have cost a fortune."

Yeah, it really did. But there's no way I was getting anything other than Rosie's dream engagement ring. It took me forever to discreetly find her inspiration board, but once I did, I had everything I needed to make it perfect for her.

"All I got was this tattoo," he says with a scoff, lifting his ring finger to show off his matching wedding band tattoo with Carter that they decided to get instead of rings.

"You told me you wanted a tattoo because it lasted forever," Carter says, dumbfounded.

James sighs. "Yeah, well, now I want jewelry."

His husband laughs, shaking his head, but then wraps his arm around James' waist, and leans down to speak against his ear. "First thing we're doing when we get back home is running to a jeweler to get you a ring," he says, holding James' hand in his.

James spins his head to face Carter, lifting his brows. "Wait. Really?" he asks. "Are you serious?"

"Yes," Carter confirms with a smile. "I love our tattoos, but if you want a ring, then you're getting a ring."

James breaks out into a smile. "I love you," he murmurs, clutching Carter's face before he leans in to kiss him.

I scoff a little at the sight. "How the hell did my proposal end with you guys deciding to buy rings?" I ask them, but they don't hear me, lost in their own world. I glance at the guys with a confused look on my face. "Should we break them up or…"

"Nah. Let them celebrate," Lucas says, with a smirk on his lips as he looks at his best friend, happy and in love. "At least it's just a kiss."

"For now," Chris chimes in with a laugh. "It's still early."

The guys laugh while James and Carter make out, and Aiden zones in on the ring. "Wow. You're really going to propose," he says with a smile.

"I am," I confirm, my own lips turning up into a smile at the thought of getting down on one knee and asking the love of my life to be my wife.

"About time," Lucas says with a laugh. "I didn't think it would take you guys this long."

"I know," I say with a sigh. "I'm happy though, and I can't wait to make her my wife."

"When exactly are you proposing?" Chris asks with narrowed eyes. "If it's this weekend, Gabi will kill you."

"He's not joking, either," Aiden says with a chuckle. "That girl will skin you alive."

I let out a scoff. "Trust me, I know," I tell the guys. "We've already had this conversation this morning, and I promised her I wouldn't steal her thunder."

"Dude. What the fuck?" Aiden says with knitted brows. "You told her before us? Before *me*?"

I shake my head. "She cockblocked me, and then gave me a lecture about Rosie, and I knew it would shut her up, and maybe she'd finally be on my side for once."

Aiden lets out a scoff, taking a sip of his drink. "Gabi, on your side?" he asks, surprise coating his tone. "I don't think I've ever seen that."

I shrug. "She told me she'd keep it a secret," I say, hoping she sticks to her word.

"And you're sure she won't tell the girls while they're out at brunch? Or the spa tomorrow? Or the bachelorette party?" Chris asks with a laugh. "I love my girl, I really fucking do, but she can't keep a secret to save her life."

I shrug. "I really don't fucking know. I hope she doesn't, or else I will steal her thunder, and propose on her wedding day."

Aiden whistles, shaking his head. "That's a death sentence, dude. Don't do it."

He might be joking, but Gabi won't be when she plunges a knife in my chest if I do end up proposing on her wedding day. "You're right," I say with a laugh. "I feel bad for the guy who ends up with her," I joke, glancing at Chris who just smiles in return.

"Are you ready?" Aiden asks Chris, patting him on the shoulder. "You're finally marrying the girl of your dreams."

"Fuck yeah," he replies with a grin. "I've been wanting to marry her for fucking years. I would have married her as soon as we graduated college, with a ring pop in the court house if that's what it took." He shakes his head in disbelief, his lips curved in a warm smile. "I can't believe it's finally happening."

I smile as I take a sip of my drink.

I can't wait to feel like that.

Chapter 4

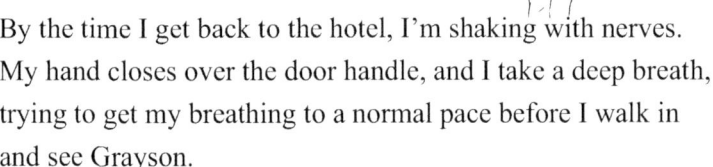

ROSALIE

By the time I get back to the hotel, I'm shaking with nerves. My hand closes over the door handle, and I take a deep breath, trying to get my breathing to a normal pace before I walk in and see Grayson.

I was a nervous wreck this morning when I found the ring in the bathroom drawer, but now that Gabi confirmed my suspicions were true, and I know what's going to happen very soon, there's no way I'll be able to contain my excitement.

As soon as I gain the courage to open the door, I see Grayson lying on top of the bed. He looks up from his phone, his face breaking out into a grin as soon as he sees me.

"Hey, angel," he says, lifting off the bed to walk toward me.

I barely have time to react before he leans down and brushes his lips against mine, so soft, so sweet. I melt into him, letting all my worries and nerves disappear as I get lost in his lips.

He pulls back, and I take a breath as his eyes zone in on mine, a smile curling his lips. "Couldn't wait to come home so I could do that," he says with a chuckle before he kisses me once, twice, three times until we get lost in each other again, and he lifts me into his arms, making my legs wrap around his waist.

I love him so much. Nine years with Grayson and I fall in love with him even more every day. I love his kisses, his touch, the way he kisses my neck and cups my breast with his hand. God, I just want to let go and lie beneath him, and let him do whatever he wants to me.

But when I remember the ring, I stiffen.

Grayson pulls back when he feels my body grow cold, and his brows dip as he searches my eyes. "Are you okay?" he asks. "Did I go too fast?"

I shake my head, pulling my bottom lip between my teeth. My body grows warm from his kind eyes on me. I love how attentive he is, how he always puts my feelings first, and always checks in with me to see if I'm okay, even after all this time.

I love him so much.

And I hate lying to him.

Which is why the nerves flowing through my body right now are obvious to him. I never lie to him. I've never kept anything from him, and now I have to hide the fact that I know what he's planning.

I'll have to wait for weeks, months, or however long it takes for him to propose, and keep lying to him as if I know nothing. The thought makes my palms feel clammy, and I'm not sure if I'll be able to hold out for that long.

"You didn't go too fast," I assure him, my heart thumping in my chest when he smiles. "I just need a glass of water. I had a little too many mimosas I think," I say with a chuckle.

His tattooed hand brushes my blonde hair behind my ear and he leans in for one more kiss. "I'll get it for you, angel," he says before heading outside of our hotel room.

I let out a breath of relief, and drop down on the bed, groaning into my hands.

I wish I hadn't found it.

I wish Gabi hadn't confirmed it was true.

Part of me is so happy that I know Grayson is planning to marry me, but an even bigger part of me wishes I was still clueless about the whole thing. Having this huge secret looming over me isn't looking good, and I don't know how long I'll have to wait before he finally asks me to marry him.

I want to marry him so bad.

I want to say yes, right now.

But I have to wait.

So, I wait, and wait, and wait, staring up at the white ceiling with bordered edges, keeping my eyes on the blank surface until Grayson bursts through the door, making me stiffen once again.

"I got you a water with no ice, and one with ice," he says, and I lift off the bed, seeing him carrying two cups in his hands. "I didn't know what you were in the mood for, so I got both," he says with a shrug.

I gulp, swallowing down the emotions building in my throat, and reach out to reach for the water with ice. I need a clear head, and the mimosas at brunch did not help. The worst thing I could do right now is lose my head and spill everything I have bottled inside of me.

Grayson eyes me while I drink the water, and his eyes narrow slightly. "Are you sure you're okay?" he asks.

I swallow down the water, placing the empty cup on the nightstand before I lift off the bed and head toward the mirror. I can't lie to him if I look at him. This way I can make myself busy. "Of course," I say, trying to keep my voice normal as I feel my heart bang against my chest.

Pumping some lotion onto my hand, I rub it on my hands, and arms, but Grayson stands behind me, and I meet his eyes in the mirror. "You're acting jumpy," he says, placing his hands on my hips, making my body freeze. "Like that."

I try to force my body to relax, but it's impossible when I meet his eyes in the mirror, and the same four words repeat themselves in my head.

I'm lying to him.

I'm lying to him.

I'm lying to him.

"What's going on, angel?" he asks, concern etched into his features.

"Nothing," I lie, swallowing hard as I pump more lotion on my hands, looking down so I don't have to lie to his face, but his thumb lifts my chin and turns my head so our eyes meet.

"Did everything go well at brunch?" he asks, arching a brow at me.

"Yep," I reply, gulping down all of my lies.

His eyes narrow slightly. "Really?" he asks, his other hand slowly caressing the side, slowly lifting my top so his palms lie flat against my stomach. A noise builds in my throat, but I swallow it back down. "Did you have any… interesting conversations?" he asks, his hand slowly lifting against my body, my top following its path.

Just that you're going to propose soon.

"Not really," I manage to say, my voice coming out a little above a whisper as his hands stop right below my breast. "Just food, drinks, Gabi being Gabi, you know."

His brow arches. "Yeah. I know what Gabi's like," he murmurs, his thumb softly grazing against my nipple over my top, making a whimper fly from my lips. "So, you guys didn't talk about anything else?" he asks, sounding more suspicious by the minute.

The more he talks, and touches me, and looks at me, the more nervous I get, and I shake my head. "Nope," I say, pressing my lips together.

His eyes squint. "Are you lying to me, Rosie?"

Crap. My lips part on a shaky breath, and my chest rises and falls with each heavy breath leaving my lips. "No," I lie.

"No?" Grayson repeats, gripping my waist in his hands before he spins me around in one quick movement so I'm looking up at him, and I'm caged in between his body and the dresser. I keep my eyes on him as he leans down and presses his lips to the curve of my neck, making my head lull back. A groan escapes him, rippling against my skin before he lifts his head, meeting my eyes. "Then why is your heart beating so fast?"

"You're… touching me," I say, feeling my body grow boiling hot as need takes over me and his brown eyes darken down at me.

"Is that the only reason?" he asks.

My heavy breaths are the only noise between us, and I blink up at him. "Yes."

Grayson lets out a low hum, his thumb softly grazing against my cheek. "I don't think that's it," he murmurs, running his nose against my jaw. "I think you're lying to me."

"I'm… I'm not," I say, hating that I'm keeping this from him.

I want to tell him. I want him to propose right here, right now. It doesn't matter where it is, as long as I'm with him. But I know the type of man Grayson is. He's the love of my life, who makes sure he searched for my dream ring. There's no way he didn't think the engagement through, and I don't want to ruin this for him.

Grayson tuts, and his grip tightens around my waist. "You've never lied to me before," he says, making my stomach drop. "So, it must be something important."

"Grayson," I start, swallowing down the nerves flowing through my body, but then he speaks, stealing the air from my lungs.

"You know about the proposal, don't you?"

Chapter 5

GRAYSON

My heart pounds against my chest the longer it takes for Rosie to say anything.

Fucking hell.

When she walked in, I was so fucking excited to see her, but I could tell something was off. She'd never been so… jumpy around me before, and yet here she was running away from me every chance she got.

My chest starts to pound as I follow her across the room, trying to figure out what had her acting so weird, until it clicked.

She knew I was going to propose.

Her lips part, and she continues looking at me with those bright blue eyes I fell head over heels for years ago, but she doesn't say anything.

"Rosie," I say, reaching out to lift her chin with my thumb. "You know, don't you?"

She starts to shake her head, ready to deny it, but as her eyes meet mine, she relents and her shoulders slump as her head moves in a subtle nod. "I know," she confirms.

Honestly, it kind of sucks that she found it before I was able to propose to her as a surprise, but I've got to say, I definitely prefer this situation over the thought of her pulling away from me for another reason.

It's been nine years with this girl. Nine fucking years of hearing her sweet, soft voice tell me she loves me, and still thinking she's way too fucking good for me, and that one day, she'll realize that, and walk right out of my life for good.

Which is why the thought of finally slipping a ring on her finger brings me an ease I can't quite explain. The idea of her being my wife, and being attached to me makes my stomach flutter like crazy.

I can't believe there was ever a time when I thought I'd be alone, or couldn't love anyone. Loving Rosalie is the easiest thing I have ever done in my life, and the best thing I've ever had the luxury of doing.

"How do you know?" I ask her, my brows dipping. "Did Gabi tell you?"

My angel bites her lip, her fair skin blushing, and for a second, my eyes drift down to that plump bottom lip pinned between her teeth, and I want to replace it with mine, kiss the daylights out of her. But I quickly shake the thought when I hear her sigh. "Well…"

"She did, didn't she?" Letting out a harsh breath, I run a hand through my hair, and groan. "I fucking knew she couldn't keep a secret. I swear to god, I'm going to—"

"No." My beautiful angel reaches out, grabbing onto my hands. I stare down at her gorgeous face, my shoulders relaxing when I meet her eyes. "She just confirmed it, but I found the ring before that. I found it this morning."

"This morning?" I repeat, my brows knitting together. "When? Where?"

"You uh…" She smirks, and the tension in my shoulders ease. I love when she smiles. "You left it in the bathroom drawer."

A light scoff escapes me. "I guess it wasn't the best hiding spot."

"Not really," she says, scrunching her nose, before her arms wrap around my waist, and she tips her head back to look up at me.

I fucking love how she fits against me so fucking perfectly. "And?" I ask her with a smile on my face as I look down at her angelic features. "What did you think?"

The pink hue returns to her cheeks, and her eyes sparkle as a smile breaks out on her face. "It's beautiful," she says. "It's exactly the one I wanted."

"I know," I confirm with a laugh, wrapping my arms around her slender waist before lowering my hands to her ass and hoist her up, her legs wrapping around me. "I didn't stalk your Pinterest for nothing."

A laugh leaves her lips and it makes my chest crack open. "How did you even know where to look?"

My lip twitch as I hold the one thing that brings me an indescribable amount of joy in this world. "I might fuck up sometimes, but when it comes to you, I'm not taking any chances. I had to make this perfect for you. I needed to know your dream ring, dress, venue… everything." Her eyes turn glassy, and my heart feels like it's about to break. I was such an idiot for ever doubting love could exist, because this right here, with her eyes on me, and my arms around her makes my chest pound so hard I feel like I'm going to die if I don't kiss her soon. "But it looks like I fucked up already," I admit, grinding my teeth together. "I should have hidden it better, or not confided in Gabi or—"

"No," Rosie interrupts, shaking her head as her soft hand cupping my face. I barely have time to smile before she leans in and presses her lips against mine in a soft, sweet kiss. Just like my angel. "You did everything right. You could never mess up."

A groan escapes my throat. "God, I can't fucking wait to marry you."

Her eyes widen, and her pretty pink lips part. "Is this—"

"No," I confirm with a laugh. "I'm not proposing right now. Partly because Gabi already threatened to cut my balls off if I stole her thunder," I start, smiling when her soft laugh makes my skin tingle. I swear she cast a spell on me with that laugh. It's the sweetest sound I've ever heard. "And partly because, we both know you deserve a million times better than a random proposal in a hotel at someone else's wedding," I tell her, arching a brow.

"How long until then?" my sweet angel asks with a grin on her face.

I can't help but laugh. I love how happy she is, how she can't wait, and the feeling is fucking mutual. "Not long," I promise her, loving when her grin widens. "But you'll still have to wait a bit. I want it to be a surprise."

I've pictured asking her to marry me for so fucking long I almost have the exact image memorized.

There's going to be flowers, hundreds, thousands of flowers, each one reminding me of her. And I can't fucking wait to make every one of her dreams come true.

"But it's coming," I promise her, dropping my forehead onto hers. "It's fucking coming, angel, and when it does, I can't wait to hear that yes."

"Yes," my girl says, eagerly.

A laugh escapes me, and I shake my head, pulling back. "Not yet," I tell her. "But I bet I could make you say yes in another way."

Her eyes light up with arousal, and I dive in, capturing her lips with mine.

Chapter 6

ROSALIE

My amazing—soon to be fiancée—kisses like no one else.

Granted, I've never actually kissed anyone else, but I don't need to. I don't need to kiss a thousand frogs, because I found my prince a long time ago, and I couldn't be happier that nine years later, we're both here, ready to get married and spend the rest of our lives together.

And I absolutely couldn't be happier when he slowly lifts my dress up and off my body, baring my breasts.

"Grayson," I gasp, when he rubs his thumb over my nipple.

His groan makes me clench as he leans in and wraps his mouth around my nipple, softly grazing the hard bud with his teeth. "I love your sweet little sounds," he murmurs, lifting his head to look at me. "Love how you open up for me. Love how you take every inch of me."

God. With every word that comes out of his mouth, I get wetter, and wetter, my legs bucking at the idea of having him inside of me.

Gently placing me on the dresser, he steps between my legs and leans down, brushing his lips with mine. "Did you bring your pretty little toy with you?" he asks, slowly peeling off my panties until I'm completely naked.

I moan into his mouth, pulling back for a second. "Which one?" I ask him, a little breathless. We've gained a collection since the first bullet vibrator he bought me in college, and Grayson loves to bring them into bed with us.

His mischievous grin makes my clit throb as he chuckles, and leans in, his lips brushing against my ear as he whispers, "The curved purple one that goes in your ass."

I gasp as her grips my ass in his hands and gives it a hard squeeze. "Yes."

A low rumble builds in his throat as he drops me to the ground and swiftly turns me around. I quickly place my hands on the dresser, dropping my head at the feel of him falling to his knees.

"This fucking ass," Grayson murmurs, rubbing the globes of my ass before spreading my cheeks, baring me to him. "I want to feel you shake around that toy while I bury my cock in this pretty little pussy."

I could come from his words alone, and I swear, I almost do. My clit aches and I buck my hips back, wanting him, needing him. "Please."

"You beg so pretty, baby," he praises, kneading the skin before I feel his lips on my ass, pressing soft kisses on my skin before his tongue replaces his lips, darting out to run over my tight hole.

"Oh god," I moan, feeling lightheaded as he continues licking softly.

A groan escapes his throat. "You like that, angel?"

"Fuck yes," I pant, losing my balance as I lean into the dresser.

"Mmmm." He continues his slow licks over my puckered hole, all while massaging the globes of my ass. "Such filthy words for such a good girl."

"God, Grayson." I tip my head back. "I need you."

He chuckles, pulling back, and I almost cry when he lifts off his knees and moves away. "Wha—" I turn my head over my shoulder, watching as he moves away.

"Hold on, angel," he says. I watch, impatiently as he pulls on the zipper of my suitcase, and pulls out the purple toy he loves. He presses the button, and the toy roars to life. Grayson's lips lift in a smirk and he turns his attention back to me. "You want it?"

I nod, slowly dying at the sound of the toy I know will be vibrating inside me soon.

"How bad?" he asks, raising his eyebrow. "How bad do you want it in your tight little ass?"

Fuck. I press my legs together, the ache getting too much to handle. "So fucking bad."

He grins, clearly satisfied with my answer. "Then bend over, angel." He lifts his chin, gesturing to the bed. "Spread open and let me ease this in."

I push myself off the dresser, heading toward the bed and lie face down, hanging off the edge of the bed.

"Such a good girl." Grayson's deep voice makes me shiver and then I feel him there, behind me, spreading my legs wider with his knees.

The distinct sound of a bottle cap rings in my ears and I shake with anticipation.

"Relax, baby," Grayson whispers, squirting some lube onto his fingers. "It's going to feel so good. I promise."

I grab a fist full of the comforter and squeeze, slowly grinding my pussy on the bed. "Please," I beg, wanting him to hurry up. As much as I love having my ass filled, I want Grayson inside me so bad, and I can't wait any longer.

His chuckle makes me even more frustrated. "So needy. Open up, baby."

I let out a deep breath, and spread myself open for him. I flinch when I feel the cool liquid touch my skin, but Grayson's hand reaches out, running all over my skin, making me ease into his touch until the toy slips past the tight muscle, and is buried inside me.

"Fuck yes," he grunts, easing it in and out of me, making me stretch around it. "You ready to turn it on?"

I open my mouth to say yes, but no noise comes out and I just nod against the bed.

"I need to hear you, angel," Grayson says, pulling out the toy a little to thrust it back inside me.

My back arches at the feel of an orgasm cresting, and I nod. "*Yes*. Turn it on."

I feel his lips press against the curve of my back before he presses the button that makes my ass buzz.

I clutch at the bed, grinding down on the fabric, needing friction so fucking bad.

"Look at you grinding that pretty little pussy on the bed. Does that feel good, angel?"

"God yes."

"Mmmm. I bet. You want me inside you?"

A noise escapes my throat as I nod, feeling the toy hit a spot deep in my ass. "Please. Fuck. Please, Grayson. Fuck me."

"You know I'm always happy to please you, angel," he says, and I hear the zipper of his jeans as he steps out of them and grabs onto my ass, spreading me wider, making the toy shift. I squeeze my eyes closed at the feel of his finger dipping inside my pussy. "You're soaking wet." He grunts, thrusting his finger deeper inside me. "So ready for me."

"Yes."

"So fucking wet, and warm, and tight."

"*Grayson.*"

He pulls his finger out of me and I barely have time to think before his cock thrusts inside, wiping the air clean out of my lungs. "Oh fuck," his deep voice makes my pussy clench around him as he pulls out and thrusts deeper inside me. "I can feel the toy inside you."

I'm so fucking full. A vibrating toy in my ass, and his cock inside me. The pleasure is so intense, I can't think, or speak, or fucking breathe. My vision goes blurry as the pleasure intensifies and deepens inside me, my bones shaking with need.

"You feel so good clenching around that toy, angel. Let me feel you come. Drench my cock, baby."

A moan flies out of my lips as I let go, and the most intense orgasm floods through me. My pussy squeezes Grayson's cock inside me as my legs shake, overstimulated by the toy. "Oh fuck. Fuck. *Fuck.*"

"That's it," he grunts, speeding up his movements. "Holy shit, this feels so fucking good." His hands fly to my hips as he thrusts me back into him until he stops, grunting as he comes deep inside of me. "Rosie. Fuck."

The feel of his cum shooting inside me has my brain melting as the buzz in my ass continues, and I drop back onto the bed, burying my head into the comforter as Grayson keeps thrusting inside me, slowly.

By the time he pulls out, I've lost track of the time, day, and year. I'm a blubbering mess, sticky and wet and utterly lost to the pleasure he gave me.

"Fuck, baby. That was so hot," he murmurs, softly shifting me onto my side.

"Mhmmm," I mumble, every thought fucked out of my head.

Grayson laughs, wrapping his arms around me to pull me onto his chest. "We need to use that toy more often."

I nod, mumbling into his chest.

Definitely.

I lift my head to look up at my boyfriend—almost fiancée—and find the only words left in my brain. "I love you."

His smile does things to me I can't explain and he leans in to press his lips to my forehead. "I love you too, angel. And I can't wait to marry you."

He dips down, brushing our lips together, before we're pulled apart by three knocks on our door, our eyes widening at the sound.

"Get your dick out of her," Gabi's voice is clear through the door. "I need to talk to Rosie."

Grayson groans, burying his head in his hands. "I'm going to fucking kill her."

The Baby

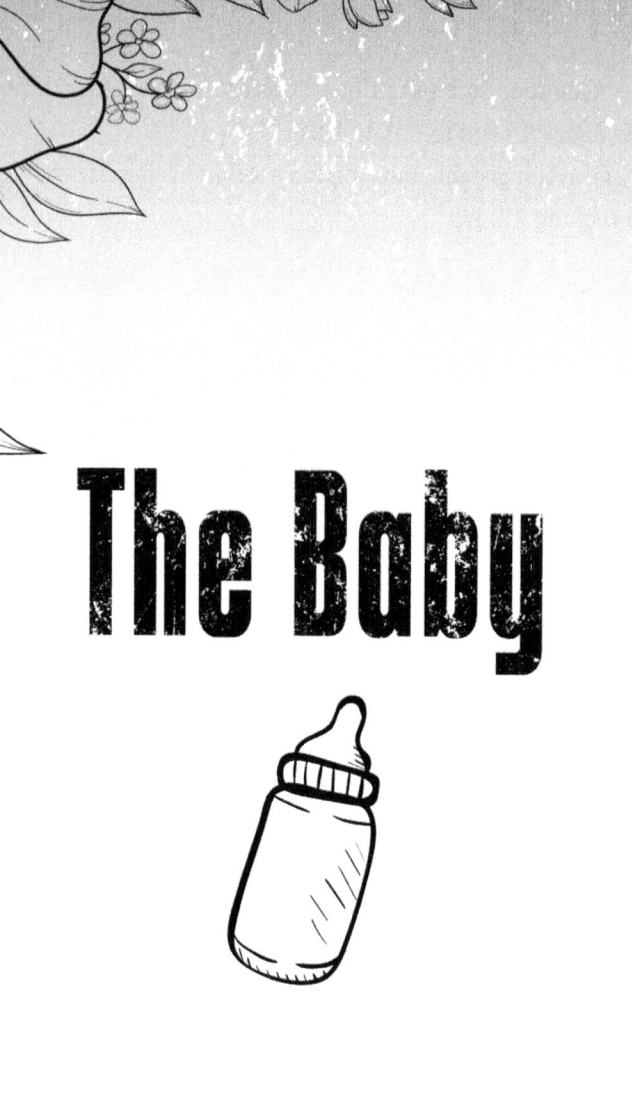

Chapter 7

LEILA

"I miss you, mommy."

My heart breaks into a million little pieces, and I press my lips together to stop the sob from leaving my lips.

"I miss you too, baby," I say to my beautiful three-year-old daughter.

I hear her mumbling, and some footsteps, and then my mother is back on the phone.

"She went to play," my mom tells me. "She reminds me so much of you at that age."

I let out a laugh. "She's so much cuter," I reply, picturing my daughter's sweet face in my mind. She has my green eyes, and her daddy's light brown hair, and cute, pink, chubby cheeks that I want to pinch all the time.

"No seas tonta," my mother says. "My daughter has always been, and still is, very beautiful."

A smile pulls at my lips. My mom and I had a long journey to get to where we are today. It wasn't always easy, and it took a lot for us to finally be in a good place, but I couldn't be happier with how our relationship is.

Growing up, I was always trying to catch up to her, always wanting to please her, to make her be proud of me, but it never worked. She always had something negative to say, a new trick to help me lose weight, or the latest diet she'd heard from a friend. She was never happy with how I looked.

It took a lot for me to finally stand up to myself and make sure she knew that what she was saying was unacceptable.

And yet, she still wasn't completely perfect. When Aiden came over to our house to meet my parents, he was a little nervous. It was so adorable. I couldn't stop smiling the whole time. This big, 6'6" basketball player that had the whole school in the palm of his hands was nervous to meet my parents.

He was shaking the whole plane ride there, constantly asking me questions about them, as if they were going to quiz him.

But when we finally got to my house and he noticed my mother watching us a little too closely—or not so subtly swapping out my food for healthier options—his nerves vanished.

He stood up for me, telling my mother off without ever raising his voice. That's something I admire about Aiden, he never loses his cool or lets anger take control. He's sweet and loves making people happy, but the moment someone hurts someone he loves, he won't stand for it.

That was a real wake-up call for her. She finally realized how much she had been hurting me, and since then, she's tried her hardest to accept me, no matter my dress size. So, hearing my mother call me beautiful now brings a tear to my eye.

"Ay, Dios mío," my mother says, her voice rising. "Nova, put my porcelain plate down right now."

The line goes quiet as she hangs up, and I let out a laugh. Nova is at the wonderful age where she wants to touch everything. And even though I love my baby girl so much, I'm kind of enjoying this little break.

I place my phone on the nightstand and lie back down in bed, turning onto my side to look at my husband. A smile tugs at my lips as I see him lying on his side, his hand resting under his head, his eyes closed, and his beautiful lips slightly parted.

My husband is the hottest man I've ever seen.

Not only is he a world-famous NBA player, desired by millions of girls and a role model to every guy out there, but he's also the best person I have ever known. He's loving, kind, and so talented that it's almost unfair.

And he's all mine.

Sometimes I can't believe he chose *me*.

My hand reaches out, and I poke at his cheek, silently wondering if this is really real.

One of his eyes snaps open, and he breaks into a smile instantly. "Morning, baby," he murmurs, his raspy voice sending a shiver down my spine as he wraps an arm around me, pulling me closer.

Even though I'm almost nine months pregnant and there's a noticeable space between us filled with our baby, Aiden doesn't seem to mind as he leans forward to kiss me.

"Were you staring at me while I slept?" he murmurs, pressing his lips against mine over and over again. "That's kind of creepy," he teases, a hint of a glint in his eye.

I let out a sigh, rolling my eyes. "I was not watching you sleep," I lie. "I just wanted to see if you were awake."

He hums, tightening his hold on my waist. "I've been awake for a while," he admits with a smirk. "Heard you on the phone to your mom."

My eyes soften. "Shit. I'm sorry. Did I wake you?"

He shakes his head. "I'd much rather be awake right now, so I can do this," he murmurs, pressing kisses all over my face.

I try not to laugh, but it's impossible when he attacks me with kisses. "What the hell are you doing?" I ask, pushing at his chest as laughter bubbles out of me.

"Taking advantage of the time we have together this weekend," he says, dipping down to kiss along my neck. "*You're my lady, my baby, and you're driving me crazy.*"

I blink in confusion, letting out a laugh. I can't say it's a normal occurrence to wake up with Aiden singing to me as he peppers little kisses all over my skin.

"Are you … singing?" I ask, my brows knitting together in confusion.

Aiden chuckles against my skin as he nods. "I've got to seduce my girl somehow."

I roll my eyes. "I'm your wife," I say. "How much more seduction could I need?"

Aiden lets out a scoff, scooching as close as he can without crushing the baby inside my belly. "Lots," he says, nuzzling his nose against my neck and kissing the sensitive skin. My lips part at the feel of him. "You're a very hard woman to please."

"Must be a horror to deal with," I reply dryly.

My husband scoffs, shaking his head. "No fucking way. It's fun working hard to hear you admit you love me and could never live without me," he says with a grin that makes me narrow my eyes.

"I'll never admit that," I say, my chest rising as my heart pounds against it.

Aiden just grins, knowing I'm lying, because we both know I love him, and he chuckles against my skin. "That just means I need to work harder for it."

"Never," I lie, tilting my head back when his mouth wraps around my nipple.

"No?" he murmurs, twirling his tongue around the hard bud.

I shake my head, but a moan spills out of my lips which makes him pull off me with a huge grin on his face. "Your mouth says one thing, but your body says another, baby." He smiles, his lips stacking above mine, only an inch away. "Tell me how much you love me," he whispers, our breaths mingling together.

A heavy breath leaves my lips, and I shake my head, pressing my lips together to stop any noises from escaping.

He arches a brow, but then his smile softens as his blue eyes lock onto mine. "That's okay. I love you enough for the both of us," he says, which makes me frown a little. He doesn't usually break this easily. He tries, and tries, and tries until I'm the one that breaks and admits to him how much I love him.

"I love you so fucking much, Leila," he says with a soft smile, cupping my face in his hand. "You're the best thing that's ever happened to me, baby."

My brows knit together, seeing his eyes sparkle as he looks at me, and I can't believe how lucky I am that he saw me one day, and wanted me. That he wants me every day. That he loves me, and our daughter.

And before I know it, the words spill out of my mouth. "Why me?"

Chapter 8

AIDEN

My wife is so fucking beautiful.

Long, gorgeous, tanned legs I love, especially when they're wrapped around my waist, or crushing my head.

Dark brown hair that spills down her back, which looks fucking amazing when it's wrapped around my fist.

Big, green eyes that make me weak in the knees.

And a beautiful face right out of my dreams.

Seriously. Someone fucking pinch me because how the fuck did I get so damn lucky?

She's the most beautiful woman in the world, even when her brows are knitted together and she has a frown on her face.

"What?" I ask, not understanding what she's asking.

She swallows hard, my eyes following the movement of her throat. "Why did you choose me?"

My face falls into a frown. "Are you … are you serious?"

My girl lets out a sigh, and rolls her eyes, turning her head away from me. "Forget it," she says. "It's stupid."

I tug on her chin to make her look at me. "Nothing you ever say or think is stupid, Leila," I tell her, searching her eyes. "What the hell brought this on?"

She avoids my eyes, and shrugs, shaking her head subtly. "I was just wondering—"

"Why I chose you?" I interrupt, my jaw ticking as her eyes land back on mine. "You think this is a carnival game and I picked a random toy?" My eyes widen a little as I look at the love of my life asking me a question that breaks my heart.

"I didn't mean it like that. I just …" She trails off, shaking her head.

"You're the love of my goddamn life, Leila," I tell her, cupping her beautiful face in my hands. "There was no choice involved. You and I were *always* meant to be."

Her long lashes blink faster than normal, the tell-tale signs that she's getting teary eyed. "We are?" she asks, her voice small and questioning.

I nod, a small smile tugging at my lips as I softly caress her cheek. "From the very first moment your lips touched mine, the choice was made for me," I admit, remembering that moment as if it was yesterday. "I never even stood a chance."

Her lips part on a breath. "But if you could choose—"

"You," I say without an ounce of hesitation, wiping the rogue tear dripping down her cheek. "It's you. Every time."

She presses her lips together, and shakes her head, letting out a hard breath. "But why?"

My brows tug together. It's been a while since she's had a moment of self-doubt, and I promised her a long time ago I'd spend the rest of my life proving to her how much I love her, and how much I need her in my life, and how gorgeous she is, but I can't help but feel my heart ache at hearing her question us.

"Have I done something to make you feel like you weren't my one and only choice?" I ask.

It's the hardest thing being away from her when I'm on the road for a game, but I can only imagine how much harder it is for her, being at home with Nova, and having to see me in the news, and on TV.

"No," she murmurs, swallowing down. "Of course not."

I shake my head, not understanding where this is coming from. "If you have to doubt how I feel about you for even a second, then …" I blow out a hard breath. "I know I haven't been home as much, and now with another baby it's going to be even harder, but …" My shoulders slump. "Maybe I should retire early or—"

"Don't even think about it," she interrupts, narrowing her gorgeous lime green eyes at me. "You're not retiring until you're old and grey, and can't move anymore." I can't help but smile a little, loving how supportive she is of my career. Of anything, really. "I'm not letting you give up your dream."

My smile widens as I trace her plump lips with the pad of my thumb, feeling my chest ache at the sight of my wife. "How many times do I have to tell you? You and the girls are my dream."

She arches a brow. "Girls?"

I shrug, laughing at her expression. "Let a guy dream," I joke, secretly hoping there's a little girl in there. Truth is, I adore the fuck out of our baby girl, Nova. Being a dad has changed me in so many ways, and I really want another baby girl that looks just like their mom.

But if Leila has a little boy, then I'll love that kid with my whole fucking heart. And who knows, maybe he'll be stubborn and bossy like his mom.

As long as they're like her, I don't mind.

I have the fucked-up genes, whereas she's… perfect.

Which makes her question hurt even more.

"Why did you ask me that, Leila?" I ask, my smile settling into something more serious. "Don't you understand that you're everything I've ever wanted?"

She parts her lips, and I can see the thoughts rambling away in that head of hers. "I'm not stupid, Aiden. I know what people think when they see us together."

My chest cracks, because *fuck*. Being in the public eye is fucking hard, especially when some people are dicks, but I really fucking hoped she wouldn't be affected by it. I hoped she wouldn't see the disgusting comments that people say, but I guess it was just wishful thinking.

"I don't care what they think," I tell her honestly. There's plenty of people that hate me, though they don't know me, and I don't give a single fuck. There was a time when I would let it eat me alive, hating the thought of someone hating me, but I've let that go a long time ago. The only person's opinions I care about is this girl right here. "You're fucking stunning baby, and anyone who says differently is blind," I tell her, wanting her to believe me when I tell her I have never seen anyone even close to being as beautiful as she is. My girl's a model for fucks sake. *I'm* the lucky one here.

She purses her lips. "I've gained weight."

I arch a brow at her. "You're pregnant."

Her green eyes glare at me, and I see them starting to get glassy which makes my stomach twist. "Stop being a smartass," she says. "I gained weight before I got pregnant with this baby, and you know it."

My brows dip as I shrug. "Okay? And that's a problem because …"

She shakes her head, frustrated. "I'm ten times bigger than the other WAG's, Aiden," she grits out.

I let out a scoff. Is she fucking kidding me? "Ten times hotter, more like."

"I'm serious," she says with narrowed eyes that turn me the fuck on.

"So am I." My eyes thin, and I shake my head, hating that she lets this silly little issue take space in her head. "You're the woman of my dreams, Leila. Stop acting like I give a shit if you've gained weight or not. Nothing is ever going to change that for me, and you know it."

"Aiden," she says, my name on her lips making me shiver.

"You're beautiful," I murmur, leaning down to kiss her lips, groaning when she melts into me, tracing her tongue over mine. "And sexy," I murmur, my tongue tangling with hers. "And so fucking hot I lose my mind."

She moans into my mouth, and I clutch her face, deepening the kiss. "Do you want me to marry you again?" I ask, barely taking a second to breathe before leaning down and kissing her again. "Do you want me to get up in front of a crowd and tell everyone all the million reasons I adore you?"

A heavy breath escapes her as she pulls back, those green eyes sparkling. "A million?"

I smirk, nodding. "Give or take."

"What are they?"

I let out a soft laugh. "Did you just trick me into complimenting you?" I tease. "Baby, you know all you have to do is ask."

Her arms wrap around my neck, and my heart feels whole. I would stay in this bed with her clinging to me forever if I could. "Tell me," she pleads.

A smile tugs at my lips as I run my thumb over her cheeks. I could sit here and compliment her all damn day. Telling her how beautiful she is, is the easiest thing in the world. "You're gorgeous, like so damn hot I can't even believe I'm lucky enough to kiss you." My chest beats with the love I have for her, and I continue. "You're the funniest girl I've ever met, and I lost my goddamn mind trying to catch up with you in college. I still do."

She smiles, knowing I'm right. Truth is, I love the chase. I love teasing her, and I love when she teases me back, making me work for an ounce of her attention.

"What else?" she asks, eagerly.

I lean down to press my lips to hers. "You're my best friend," I murmur, dropping my forehead onto hers. "I can't imagine my life without you in it." My breaths come out heavy, and I let out a sigh. "I need you so much that I can't understand how I ever lived twenty years before you." Her soft hands slide up, getting lost in my hair. "And I'm so fucking grateful you decided to make a life with me." My throat bobs as I shake my head. "You gave me a family, and showed me what love is like." Tears build in my eyes, and my girl reaches up, wiping them away, as her own eyes start to tear up. "And you're the best mother to Nova. She loves you so much, and so do I, baby. So fucking much."

I don't even catch a breath before I clutch her face and kiss her, getting lost in her lips until she opens up for me. I know she gets in her head sometimes, but I will always show her how much I love her. I've spent the last eight years doing just that, and I'll continue to do so until my last breath.

"That was only five things," she points out when she pulls back from the kiss.

A laugh bubbles out of me and I shake my head. "A million is a *lot*," I say, blowing out a breath. "Good thing we have the rest of our lives for that." She laughs, the sound hitting me right in the chest. It's my favorite thing in the whole entire world. I break out into a grin, staring down at my favorite eyes. "You make me so happy, baby. You have no idea how much. Our life is... perfect."

"Perfect?" Leila questions, her eyes searching mine.

"Perfect," I confirm with a grin, kissing her again. "Just like you, baby."

She smiles, shaking her head. "God, you're so cheesy. Why did I ever marry you?"

She's such a tease. Loves to annoy me, and pretend she hates me when I know she loves me. Not as much as I love her—that would be impossible—but pretty damn close.

"Because you love me," I tell her, softly kissing her.

"I don't."

I grin, loving when she teases me. "No?" I ask, leaning over her on my elbows so I don't crush our baby. My hand finds her bare pussy under the sheets, and I groan when I find what I knew I would. "Then why are you so wet?"

She doesn't answer, knowing I'm right, and widens her legs, making room for me.

I chuckle, settling myself over her. "So needy, baby." My cock runs over her pussy, teasing her sensitive clit. My girl gets so horny while she's pregnant, and I love indulging her every need. "You want me inside you?"

A groan leaves her. "Just fuck me already."

I tut, shaking my head. "Manners, baby. Use them."

She groans, bucking her hips, grinding herself over my aching cock. "Fuck me," she pleads. "Please, Aiden."

Her name on my lips makes my bones shake, even after all these years. "Tell me how much you want my cock," I repeat. I let her get away with it earlier, but this time, I'm not stopping until I hear the words from her pretty little mouth.

Her gorgeous green eyes turn into slits as she narrows them at me. "I'm not indulging your ego."

"Shame," I sigh, torturing both myself and her when I thrust against her clit, instead of inside her like we both want. "Guess you'll have to take care of this pretty pussy by yourself."

I move away from her, grinning down when I see her chest rising with harsh breaths. "I want it," she says through gritted teeth.

"What's that?" I tease.

A sigh escapes her lips and she closes her eyes for a second before she reaches for me, gripping my cock in her fist. "I want your cock inside of me."

Oh fuck. Her fist tightens around my dick, jerking me and I lose all consciousness of whatever the fuck it is I asked her.

"Fuck me, Aiden. *Please.* I need my husband to fuck me."

A groan builds in my throat at that word, and I slap her hand away, replacing it with mine as I press my cock against her entrance. I don't hesitate before thrusting deep inside my wife, making her moan loud enough for the whole hotel to hear.

"You're playing dirty," I whisper against her lips as I thrust my cock deeper inside her.

"You wouldn't give me what I wanted," she pants as I slide deeper inside her pussy, feeling her grip every inch of me inside her.

Little shit. My eyes squeeze shut with the pleasure running through me, and I cup her breast in my hand, squeezing it.

"Oh fuck. I'm so close."

I almost laugh. I know how sensitive her gorgeous tits are when she's pregnant, and I'm using it to my advantage. Her pussy grips my dick inside of her as I fuck her faster, wanting, dying to feel her flood my cock.

"God yes," I grunt, my cock twitching inside of her. "Come baby. Let me feel you."

She throws her head back, and her pussy convulses as the orgasm hits her. I try to hold on. Fuck, I really do, but it's impossible when she tightens around me again.

A moan leaves my lips as I thrust inside of her, and come inside of her tight pussy, my soul leaving my body as the orgasm falls over me.

I keep thrusting slowly, as we both come back down from the high, and finally pull out. My cock twitches when I see my cum dripping out of her. It's not like she can get pregnant twice.

I fall onto the bed, my breathing slowing down. "Fuck." That ended quicker than I expected, but after having a kid, and barely having time to see her, there's no way it's ending here. I'm fucking my girl until her legs shake.

Leila turns on her side, and cups my face in her hands. I twist on my side to face her, seeing my favorite person in the world. "Knew I could get you to fuck me," she says with a smirk, leaning down to kiss me before she turns around and lifts herself off the bed.

I really try to focus on her face. I do. But I fail immediately, my eyes roaming over her perfect tits, and smooth, golden skin, her belly plump with my baby.

God damn.

She gets more beautiful every year.

I can't help but let out a laugh. She knows exactly what she does to me whenever she calls me her husband.

It drives me fucking insane.

The first time she did it, was during our honeymoon. I fucked her for hours until we were both on the verge of passing out.

And that's how Nova happened.

Honestly, no regrets. A million out of Ten. Would do it again.

My smile widens as I watch her walk toward the bathroom, her ass jiggling with every step she takes. A groan leaves my lips when I feel my cock harden at the sight, and she glances behind her shoulder for a second before walking inside.

I let out a laugh noting the bathroom door left open, which she does whenever she wants me to join her.

My sweet, beautiful wife.

Pretends she hates me, but is so needy for my cock.

I lift off the bed to join her, and give her what she needs when my phone rings on the nightstand with a text, and my smile drops as I glance down at the screen.

I hate hiding things from Leila. I did it once, and it was the worst mistake I have ever made.

I share everything with her, and I want to tell her.

And I will soon, but… I don't know how she's going to take it.

I swipe away the notification and shake it off, deciding to tell her soon, and walk into the bathroom, seeing my beautiful wife in the shower, holding the shower head to her pussy, soft moans leaving her lips.

She glances back at me when she hears me, and her eyes blink. "You took too long. I started without you."

I chuckle, wiping my mouth. As I said…

Luckiest guy in the world.

I pull open the glass door, and walk into the shower, grabbing the shower head from her hands. "Lean back against the wall, and open your legs, baby. Let me show you how good your *husband* is at taking care of you."

Chapter 9

My chest warms when I hear the bathroom door open, and my husband walks out with a towel wrapped around his waist. My eyes drop to his smooth pale skin, rippled with muscles everywhere.

His blue eyes shine when he sees me, his lips spreading out into a grin. "Holy fuck, gorgeous. Where the fuck do you think you're going dressed like that?"

I love Aiden's eyes on me. I loved them the first time he ever looked at me, and I love them now, eight years, and one and a half babies later.

But I also love teasing him, so I smirk as I hold his gaze in the mirror when I say, "The girls and I are going to a strip club tonight."

His bright blue eyes darken as he narrows them at me, and lets out a low groan, wrapping his arms around my waist. "I know that's bullshit," he whispers against my skin, pulling me back into him. "I already warned Gabi about strippers and she assured me there wouldn't be any." *Dammit.* "But I also know why you're teasing me. I know you want *this*." His lips find my neck and I melt against him. "You want me to be jealous and stake my claim on you, don't you?" I open my mouth to retort when his hands find my belly, and he rubs it, making me glance down. "I'm jealous as fuck of any man who puts their eyes on you. But I know I don't need to be. This this baby is mine," he says, licking the length of my neck, drifting down to my hands until he rubs my wedding band between his fingers. "And you're mine."

"I'm not." My voice comes out as a breath.

"You are," he murmurs, twisting me around to press his lips to mine. "And I'm yours," he whispers, before cupping my face and kissing me so deep I can't think of anything else. "No matter where I go, no matter who the fuck is around me." My breath hitches. "All I see is you."

His tongue swipes against mine and I melt into him, wrapping my arms around his neck. I love this man so much, and I love that he knows how I feel without ever opening my mouth.

I hate seeing other women thirst after Aiden, completely disregarding our relationship. It breaks my heart when I see it in person, and it's even worse when he's at away games and I make up a million and one scenarios in my head.

But I also trust him, and I know he loves me more than anything in the world, aside from our daughter and his baby that I'm carrying.

I let out a deep breath when he pulls back and presses his forehead against mine. "You know you don't have to worry, right?" he asks, his eyes searching mine. "I will never look at anyone but you. I will never *want* anyone but you."

I gulp, unable to look away from his eyes. "I know." I really do. Even if I get jealous sometimes, and feel self-conscious, I know the kind of man Aiden Pierce is. "It's just… hard," I admit. "Being away from you all the time. Every time you're gone…"

His lips press against my forehead, lingering on the skin. "I know. It's so fucking hard for me too, gorgeous. I wish you could come with me to all my games, but I know you can't. I know that." He sighs against my hair. "You're an amazing mom, and I know Nova needs you with her." We've tried nannies before, once, but I couldn't bear the thought of leaving my kid with someone else. "And Nova definitely can't spend all her time on planes and in hotels." Aiden pulls back, looking me in the eyes. "And when she comes around, it's going to be even harder," he says, glancing down at my belly.

I roll my eyes, a smile curling my lips. "You've got to stop saying *she*. What if it's a boy?"

He just grins, kissing me once more. "It's not."

He's so certain, it makes me want to laugh. The group all have bets on what the gender is going to be, and while I bet it would be a boy, I wouldn't mind losing a hundred bucks if it means Aiden is happy.

I want to be his happiness. I want our family to be the family he never had. Show him how good life can be when he has a real family who cares about him like Nova and I do.

"Fuck, you really do look good." Aiden's eyes drift down my body, his hands mapping out everywhere his eyes look. "Are you sure you need to go out today?" he asks with a mischievous smile.

I swat his hands away, turning back around to face the mirror. "The girls booked a spa day. Gabi wants to get pampered before the bachelorette tonight."

He groans, clutching my hips in his hold. "You better behave," the rumble in his voice makes me shiver.

64

"It's just a spa day." I blink innocently up at him. "How much trouble can I get in?"

His teeth nip at my neck, making me gasp. "You know that's not what I meant." His lips press against my skin, soothing the bite. "If I find out Gabi lied to me about the strippers…"

A knock hits our hotel door, and Aiden looks up. "Hello? We're waiting."

I turn around to walk toward the door, but Aiden halts me with his hand wrapped around my wrist. "I love you."

My eyes soften, and I flash him a smile. "I love you, too."

I barely walk out of the room when I hear, "You look like you've just been fucked."

Well, what a way to meet my friends.

"Gabi," Madi chastises.

"What?" Gabi says, shrugging. "She does."

"I do?" I ask the girls, smoothing out my hair.

Madi sighs, shaking her head, but then she tilts her head and purses her lips together. "A little."

I roll my eyes. *Great.*

"You're about to pop," Gabi says. "Is that even safe?"

I let out a laugh. "I can't wait until you get pregnant. Chris's dick will fall off." Gabi looks confused, wondering, and I turn to Rosie. "Help me," I plead.

She smiles, approaching me to wipe the smudged makeup around my mouth, and fix my hair. "There."

"Your lipstick's still a little smudged," Gabi points out. "Couldn't you have waited until we got back home?"

"Give me a break," I say as we walk down the hallway. "I don't see Aiden often, and this is the one chance we have of being together without Nova being there."

"Children are such cockblocks," Gabi says. "Have you thought of asking your mom to take her more often?"

I let out a laugh. "And basically paint the picture that Aiden and I are going to be fucking while she takes my baby? No, thank you."

Gabi shrugs. "Just a thought."

A smile pulls at my lips as I glance at her. "How about you take her?" I joke.

"Me?" Gabi asks, her eyes so wide they look like they're about to fall out.

I laugh. "I'm only joking. You wouldn't know the first thing about babies."

The girls laugh, but then Gabi stops abruptly, keeping her eyes on mine. "What if… what if I wanted to?"

I lift an eyebrow. "You want to babysit Nova?"

She nods. "I love that little girl, you know I do."

Yeah, she does. Gabi is the best auntie to our baby. She spoils her like crazy, and while I was joking about Gabi watching Nova, it seems like it's something she actually wants to do.

"If you want to watch Nova for a few hours while Aiden's home, then that's fine by me," I say with a shrug.

Her face lights up, breaking out into a grin. "Wait. Really?" she asks. "You really trust me with her?"

I let out a soft chuckle at her reaction. "Of course, I do, Gabi."

Her smile widens and she reaches over, and wraps her hand around my arm, giving it a soft squeeze.

I blink, confusion etched on my face. "What the hell was that?" I ask her.

"A sign of affection," she says, rolling her eyes. "Obviously."

I arch a brow, pressing my lips together in amusement. "Squeezing my arm is showing me affection?"

"Yes." Gabi frowns. "What else did you want me to do? Make out with you to show you I'm thankful?"

I let out a laugh. What a weirdo. God, I love her. "No," I say, shaking my head. "An arm squeeze is more than enough."

"Exactly," she says, flicking her hair behind her shoulder. "Let's go, or we'll be late."

Madeline lets out a scoff. "Since when do you care about being late?"

Gabi looks behind her shoulder with a smirk. "Since I booked a whole spa treatment before the bachelorette tonight."

"How long is this going to take, exactly?" Madi asks.

"Just a few hours," Gabi says, waving a hand as she pushes the door open. "Wedding planning has been hard as hell. I deserve this."

We let out a laugh, following her into the spa, looking around. The air smells like fresh cucumbers, and the quiet, soothing music makes my shoulders dip, relaxation already taking over.

"And so do you," Gabi says, nudging my arm. "I know you're tired, and stressed, so I booked you a massage."

"You did?" I arch a brow. "Wow… that's nice."

"I know," Gabi says with a smile. "If only I had a friend like myself."

I let out a scoff, and lift my head when I see a lady walking toward me, flashing me a smile.

"Have fun, and try not to moan too loud. I'm getting a massage right next door."

I let out a laugh, following the lady into the room, and as soon as I lie on the table, and her hands start working my muscles, I let out a groan that's undoubtedly loud enough for Gabi to hear.

God. I underestimated how much I needed this. Some quiet time to relax, and be pampered.

I adore Nova. She's the best thing that ever happened to me, along with her father, but being a mom is hard, especially to a three-year-old. And now with another on the way, I'm tired. All the goddamn time. Aiden helps a lot when he's home, but when he's not, it's just me and her, and I miss him all the time.

"Oh my god, *yes*! Right there, Petra. Get those knots out."

I scrunch my eyebrows, hearing Gabi's voice next door, and let out a laugh.

And she told *me* not to be too loud.

Chapter 10

AIDEN

My eyes tear away from the TV as soon as the door opens, and Leila walks inside, my lips lifting into a huge grin at the sight of her. Four years of being married to the most beautiful girl in the world, and I still smile like a fool whenever I see her.

Leila trails inside, her eyes hooded as if she's just woken up from a deep sleep, and she hums as she walks toward me, joining me on the bed.

"Hey, baby," I say, turning the TV off as I slide my hands to her face and bring our lips together. The scent of massage oil enters my noise and I hum into her mouth, loving how sweet she smells, though I prefer the usual peach scent from her shampoo.

She moans into my mouth, her lips lifting into a smile against mine. "Mmm. Hi," she replies, her eyes fluttering as she melts into me, wrapping her arms around my neck.

"Jesus," I say with a chuckle, pulling away to hold her face in mine, seeing her smile, and look dreary. "What the hell did they do to you in there?"

She hums again, letting out a soft, content sigh. "They took all my stress away," she replies.

I arch an eyebrow, feeling a tinge of possessiveness in me. Kinda getting jealous that someone put their hands all over her body and made her *this* happy. "You don't need them to do that. I can take your stress away, gorgeous," I tell her, bringing out lips together.

She laughs, shaking her head. "Sorry, but it was better than orgasms."

"Really?" I ask, smirking at her. "Want me to remind you how good my orgasms are?"

She lets out a chuckle, resting her head on mine. "Yes, please."

My lip twitch at the sight of her so soft, and fucking adorable. "I've got to say, I kind of like this version of mellowed out Leila," I say, pressing my lips to her cheek. "But I love when you tease me more," I admit with a smirk.

"I don't have the energy for that," she murmurs with a sweet sigh. Her eyes flick open and she runs her hands up my arms, reaching my face as she traces her fingers over my brows before running her hands through my hair. "You're so beautiful."

Seeing her smile, and touch me, and compliment me makes a shiver run up my spine. "Holy shit," I breathe out a laugh, wrapping my arms around her waist as I bring her closer to me. "I'm going to book you a massage every fucking week if it makes you like this," I joke, feeling her soft hair beneath my fingers as I brush it behind her ear.

She shakes her head, her gorgeous green eyes that knocked the air out of my chest when I first met her hood as a smirk appears on her lips. "You're acting like I'm drunk. I'm just complimenting my husband."

That word on her lips, makes me groan as I bring our lips together and I kiss her, with every ounce of love I have for her.

"I love you," I mumble against her lips, going back for another kiss, and another, and another. Can't get enough of my wife.

She hums, smiling against my lips. "Love you," she says, kissing me back.

Fuck. I want to tell her. I don't like keeping things from her, and I want to just come out and tell her, and let her in on the secret that's had me going out of my mind for days now. But I also don't want to stress her out.

She's so tired and stressed from taking care of Nova, and she rarely has time to just relax. And here she is, bordering on drunk from being relaxed. I can't ruin this.

"You're thinking," she mumbles against my lips, pulling back with an arched brow. Her hands run through my hair and she leans in to press her lips against my cheek. "Want to tell me what's going on?"

I let out a laugh, feeling my heart pump in my chest. "You know me so well," I muse, loving that my wife just knows when something's up.

She sighs, shrugging. "I fell in love with you. I had to." A chuckle bubbles out of me, loving how she continues to tease me. "What are you thinking about?" she asks.

My smile slips, and the muscle in my jaw ticks. "I'll tell you another time."

But Leila doesn't let it go, narrowing her eyes. "Why?"

"Because, gorgeous," I say, smoothing my hands over her waist. "I don't want to do anything that might make you lose this bliss," I tease with a smirk.

But the previously mentioned bliss leaves her as soon as those words are out of my mouth, and she stiffens, furrowing her brows. "What is it?" she demands, her brows knitting together.

"Another time, baby," I tell her. "Let's just enjoy the time we have together." I lean in to kiss her, but Leila pulls back, her frown deepening.

"You never keep secrets from me," she says, almost accusingly and I hate that she's thinking the worst now.

"I know," I reply with a sigh. "And I don't want to. I want to tell you."

"Then tell me," she says, dropping her hands from my hair. Her expression hardens, and I breathe out a sigh.

"My mom reached out."

Leila's eyes widen, and she purses her lips. "When?"

"A week ago?" I say with a shrug.

She blinks a couple of times, her brows knitting together. "A week?" she repeats as if the words are foreign.

I nod, running my hands down the soft skin of her arms. "I wanted to tell you sooner, I just… didn't know what to do," I admit. I haven't talked to her in a long time. A long, long time. She was a big part of my horrible childhood, and it made me wary of talking to her when all she had done was put me through hell. But… I've always had a sliver of hope she'd want to reach out. And now she has.

"What did she want?" Leila asks, tensing up. I almost smile, loving how she cares so much about me. I fucking love her for that.

"She's sober," I tell her. Leila's eyes widen, and I continue. "Cameron told me she went to rehab, and has been sober for six months now."

Leila's brows dip, and I understand her reaction. My brothers and my mother have never been trustworthy, especially when my brother Brandon had threatened me for money after I got into the NBA. I had cut them off way before then, but after that, I decided not to ever even think about them.

Until one day, Cameron showed up at my door, crying, and begging me to help him, telling me he'd go to rehab if needed. I was apprehensive at first. They'd never wanted to be sober before. At first, I thought both of my brothers were in on it, wanting to scam me out of my money.

Until he told me Brandon had died of an overdose.

He fucking died.

My brother died and I didn't even know.

It felt like my heart had been ripped out of my chest when I saw my brother, my only brother now, at my door crying, begging me to save him so he wasn't next.

I couldn't say no.

I helped him, took him to the best rehab I could find, and kept in touch with him until he left a new man.

I'd never seen Cameron like that. Clean, sober, happy.

But my mom… she didn't want to be helped.

So, when Cameron told me she paid for rehab herself, and has been sober for six months, I was skeptical, too.

"Six months isn't a long time," Leila points out.

I nod in agreement, a sad smile on my lips. "It's longer than I've ever seen her sober my whole life," I admit to her, my heart breaking for my younger self, having to see my mom like that, day in, day out. Every. Single. Fucking. Day.

Leila's eyes soften, and I see a hint of sadness in them. I've told her everything I've been through as a kid, but she can't even begin to fathom the reality of living it.

"Have you gone to see her yet?" she asks.

"No." I shake my head. "Of course not. I wanted to talk to you about it first."

She blinks. "Me?"

"Of course, baby," I say, cupping her face. "You're my wife. This is our life. Yours, mine, and Nova's." Her eyes flutter closed at the feel of my palm on her cheek. "This affects all of us. Not just me," I clarify. "If I reach out, then she'll be in our lives." I breathe out a sigh. "What should I do?" I ask her.

Leila's brows dip. "You're asking me?"

I nod. "I want to know what you think," I admit.

Her lips part on a sigh. "Do you want her in your life?" she asks me.

My brain says the word over and over again until I nod. I've always had a soft spot for her. A special place for her in my heart that was always vacant. Empty. *Abandoned*. "I think so."

Leila nods in understanding, and clutches my face between both her hands. "She hurt you," she says, concern etched on her face.

"I know," I say with a nod. "But she's my mom."

Leila softens and she nods, knowing that I need this. Want this. Leila had issues with her mom when she was growing up, and since they fixed their issues, they've been pretty close, and she's an amazing grandma to Nova.

I want that. All I've ever wanted was a relationship with my mom, and for years, she just wanted me gone.

But she wants me now.

And I don't want to turn from that.

"And you're sure she's sober?" Leila asks.

"I mean, I'm not completely sure," I admit, since I haven't seen her with my own eyes yet. "But Cameron said she's doing really well." My heart swells at the thought.

Leila leans down and brushes her lips against mine, kissing me softly. "I think you should do what you want," she says, placing her hand against my heart. "You've got a big heart, Aiden, and if you want to share it with her, then I'll support you the whole time."

Fuck. My throat closes up and I shake my head. "I love you," I tell her, unable to express my feelings for her in any other way. I'd buy her the fucking moon if I could.

"I love you, too," she says with a smile that makes my heart flutter like crazy.

This woman still gives me butterflies.

Even after being married to her for four years.

"I don't know why I was so scared to talk to you about it," I admit with a laugh. I should have known she'd be supportive. She's the best fucking person in the whole world.

"I think you were scared I'd tell you it was a bad idea," she says with a shrug. "She really hurt you, but you've always wanted her approval."

I guess a part of that is true. There was a time in my life when I just wanted her to look at me. To love me. But that was a long time ago.

"I want your approval more," I tell my wife, getting lost in her lime green eyes.

Leila scoffs. "Sure."

"I'm serious," I tell her, my brows dipping. "You could tell me to cut her off for good, and I'd do it, Leila. Nothing means more to me than you do. You've been my family for a hell of a lot longer than she ever was."

Leila's beautiful eyes soften. "I'd never tell you to do that."

"I know," I say with a smile as I kiss her pretty, pink lips. "And that's why I love you, gorgeous." I waste no time, wrapping my arm around her waist and gently flip us over so she's lying on the bed and I'm crowding her, spreading her legs with my thighs.

Her breathing speeds up, and when I pull away from her lips, her eyes are hooded with lust.

"Please," she begs, arching her back to grind her pussy over the bulge in my pants. "I need you."

I'm already pulling my pants down my legs, and throw them across the room, zoning in on her spread legs, and pull her dress up her body so she's bare beneath me, her belly swollen with my child and her beautiful body on display for me. "Fuck. Just look at you, baby," I tell her, slowly stroking my cock as I just look at her.

So fucking gorgeous.

Jesus, I'm a lucky bastard.

"Please," she repeats, reaching for me. "You need to hurry up. The bachelorette party is in an hour."

A groan slips my lips as I rip my shirt off, and kneel between her legs, my thumb rubbing circles over her pretty little clit. "Let me take care of you, baby. There's no need to rush me. We have all the time in the world."

"Until she gets here," Leila says, running a hand softly over her belly. "She'll be here soon, and then you won't be able to have me for six weeks," she points out with a smirk.

I arch a brow. "I can still make you come without sticking my dick in you," I tell her, thrusting a finger inside her until her back arches. Fuck. She's so wet, and tight, and I can't wait to fuck my wife.

"You can't even handle six weeks?" Leila asks, shaking her head, a moan spilling out of her lips as I position my cock against her entrance, rubbing it over her clit. "You can't live without me, huh?"

I smirk at her teasing and shake my head. "I really can't," I say, sliding home.

Chapter 11

LEILA

"Oh fuck." I lift my head, seeing Gabi fall into the booth beside me, immediately dropping her head on my shoulder. "I feel like I'm gonna pass out."

A laugh bubbles out of me as she squeezes her eyes closed, and the girls all smile in amusement at ger state. "You might want to go easy," I suggest, knowing it's no use since the chance of her listening to me is slim to none.

She shakes her head, her face screwing up. "No fucking way," she says, lifting her head, and squaring her shoulders. "This is my bachelorette party, I'm not going to sit around and *rest*." She makes a disgusted expression, and lifts out of the booth, tugging on my hand. "Come on. You're coming to dance with me."

My brows tug together because… I really do not want to get up on that dancefloor and dance when I'm about to pop. "Why not Madi or Rosie?" I ask her, subtly widening my eyes at the girls, begging them to take my place.

Gabi, however, shakes her head. "Rosie can't dance," she says, casting an apologetic look at Rosie, "sorry, but it's true." Rosie raises her brows in shock, but Gabi continues. "And Madi's already been out there with me, but you haven't."

My eyes narrow down at her. "Did you forget I'm pregnant?" I ask, raising my brow at her. "I can't move like you," I say, gesturing to my protruding belly.

She shoots me a dry look. "If you can fuck your husband all damn day, then you can dance a little at my bachelorette party."

Damn it. "Fine," I huff, sliding out of the booth—not well, might I add—until I stand, and barely have time to catch my breath before Gabi tugs me onto the dancefloor, hundreds of people moving to the beat of the music, surrounding me.

"Come on," Gabi says, spinning around to face me before her hands drift to my hips. "Move your hips, grandma. Have some fun. You need this."

My eyes narrow down at her. "Who the hell are you calling a grandma?"

Gabi snickers, a glint shining in her eyes. "You're right. My grandma can dance better than you."

I let out a scoff, and start to move my hips to the music like she instructed me to, because the girl is bossy as hell, and won't stop pestering me until she gets what she wants.

The music is good, and the room is dark and loud, and it's pretty fun.

Until someone bumps into me, and I'm reminded of why I hate places like this. A groan leaves my lips when I'm pushed toward Gabi, and I squint down at her. "I'd much rather be lying in bed smothered by snacks right now."

She laughs a little, and rolls her eyes. "Sounds so fun," she says, sarcasm dripping from her tone.

"Maybe not for someone like you," I tell her with a shrug. "But for someone who's pregnant, and dying to take a nice hot bath, it sounds like a dream."

Gabi keeps her eyes on me for a second, and then lets out a sigh. "It's just… this is the last time I'll get to do something like this," she says. "I want to enjoy it."

My brows dip in confusion. "What the hell are you talking about?" I ask her. "You're getting married, not dying." When she shoots me a look, I let out a laugh, and continue. "Besides, Rosie will be getting married soon, and you'll have her bachelorette party to attend."

Gabi lets out a scoff. "Please. We both know her bachelorette party is going to be big, and expensive and beautiful just like she is. I just wanted one last night to have fun in a trashy, loud club with my girls," she says, her expression sincere as her lips curl into a smile.

I place my arm on her shoulder. "I promise this won't be the last time you get drunk and dance in a club," I tell her. "And I'd love to do that with you another time, but right now… I need to sit down," I say with a mixture of a groan and a cry. "My feet are hurting, and I'm tired, and… *please*."

Gabi snickers, and looks behind my shoulder, making me turn around. Rosie smiles at us, and flashes me a wink. "Madi went to the bathroom, and I'm bored. So, I'm taking over," she says, holding a glass with pink liquid as she moves to the beat—badly, very, very badly—but Gabi doesn't seem to mind, letting out a laugh as she grabs Rosie's hand.

"Thank you," I mouth, letting out a heavy breath before heading back to the empty booth, my feet throbbing when I finally sit down.

My head snaps to the side when I hear a buzzing, and reach into my bag, seeing Aiden's name flashing on the screen. My lips immediately turn into a smile when I open his text, reading the words over and over again.

Aiden:

> I miss you like crazy

I let out a laugh as I quickly type out a text, and hit send.

Leila:

> I was with you less than an hour ago.

Aiden:

> And that's way too fucking long. Please tell me you can come see me? I need to kiss you.

A smile spreads across my face, and I lift my head, searching the crowd until I see Gabi and Rosie dancing together, both of them looking as drunk as each other. Letting out a laugh, I lower my head, and type out a text.

Leila:

> If you think Gabi will let me leave her bachelorette party, you really don't know her.

Aiden:

> You can sneak out like we used
> to do when we first got together.

My smile widens at the memories of being a sophomore and sneaking around with Aiden Pierce. Secret hookups, and having to hide it in front of our friends was kind of fun, like we had our own little world whenever we were together. It's still so crazy how far we've come since then, how back then, I never could have imagined I'd be married to the man of my dreams and carrying his second child.

Leila:

> We're too old for that now. And I'm
> too pregnant to be sneaking around.

Aiden:

> Don't give me that bullshit, gorgeous.
> We're not even thirty yet. Don't make
> me feel like a middle-aged dad.

Leila:

> But you are a dad. The best dad.

Aiden:

> And I'm still young. We're still
> young and fun, and I want to see you
> right fucking now.

I tug my bottom lip between my teeth, my smile widening with each second I stare at his message.

Aiden:

> Come on, baby. I really fucking miss
> you. Just let me kiss you for a bit, and
> then you can go back.

His offer is tempting as hell, and I can't pretend that the idea of sneaking around isn't fun, but when I see Madi walking toward the booth, I know I can't leave.

I love Aiden, but this night is for my girls. No matter how tired I am, I'm sticking around with my girls.

Leila:

> I can't. Sorry. See you tonight.
> I'll make it worth it.

Aiden:

> You're torturing me, baby.

Leila:

You still love me, though.

Aiden:

That, I fucking do.

"Was that Aiden?" Madi asks, sliding into the booth in front of me when I place my phone back into my purse.

I nod, letting out a sigh. "He wanted me to sneak out to meet up with him," I admit.

A laugh spills out of her lips as she arches a brow. "Gabi would never let that happen."

I shake my head, laughing. "I know," I agree. "Why the hell did I think we would have a mellow night, tonight?"

Madi shakes her head, reaching out to grab her drink before taking a sip. "At least there aren't any strippers," she points out with a smirk.

"Yet," I reply with a shake of my head. "The night is still early, and I'm already really tired."

"I bet," she says, a soft laugh leaving her as her eyes drift down to my belly. Her smile slips as she keeps her eyes on it, and my brows furrow.

"Is everything okay?" I ask her, wondering why she's staring at my belly so hard. I glance down, trying to see if there are any stains. "Do I have something on my clothes, or—"

"No," Madi says with a chuckle. "No. I was just wondering."

"About?" I ask her.

She holds eye contact for a while, and then lets out a sigh. "What is it like being pregnant?"

Ah. I can see how much Madi and Lucas want kids, and the fact that it hasn't happened for them yet, when I'm already on my second, must be hard.

"Horrible," I say, trying to lighten the mood. Madi laughs at my answer, and arches a brow, knowing I'm lying. "I'm kidding. It's amazing," I admit with a sigh. "Having my baby growing inside of me is inexplicable. I love feeling her grow and turn into a little human."

"Her?" Madi asks with a smirk.

"Damn it," I groan, my eyes fluttering closed. "It's all Aiden's fault. He's convinced the baby is a girl, and now apparently has me saying it's a girl, too."

"I actually think it'll be a girl, too," she says with a smile.

I roll my eyes. "Am I the only one who bet on the baby being a boy?"

She shakes her head, her dark brown skin glistening from the lights in the club. "No. I think Grayson did, too," she says. "So, you want a boy?"

I let out a sigh. "I don't know," I admit. "I kind of wanted to see a little boy with Aiden's features. Bright blue eyes, soft brown hair, and I'd love to see him wear a basketball cap like his dad," I admit with a smile, imagining it. "But two girls… It's going to be really hard, especially with Aiden being away so often."

Madi smiles reassuringly, and reaches out to squeeze my hand. "You're going to do great no matter what," she says. "You're an amazing mother, Leila. Nova is adorable, but not only that, she's kind, and respectful, and the best part of you both."

My heart squeezes. Even though it's been hard sometimes, raising Nova to be the girl she is today has been amazing, and I wouldn't exchange it for anything in the world.

"Thank you," I say, squeezing her hand. "I think I really needed to hear that. Aiden tells me how amazing I'm doing with her all the time, but sometimes I wonder if it's just because he wants in my pants," I joke, letting out a laugh.

A scoff leaves her lips, and she shakes her head. "You know damn well that guy is crazy head over heels for you, and he'd stay celibate for the rest of his life if it meant he got to keep you."

I let out a groan, my face screwing up. "God forbid," I say with a shake of my head.

Madeline lets out a laugh, her head turning to the side when she sees Gabi approaching us, Rosie following her.

"You guys are still sitting here?" Gabi asks.

"We're resting," Madi replies, dryly. "It's what *normal* people do."

I lift my head when I hear Rosie blowing a raspberry. "Normal is boring," she says, slurring her words.

"Oh boy," I say with a laugh. "Grayson's gonna have a hell of a time dealing with drunk Rosie."

"I'm not drunk," Rosie replies with a frown.

Gabi chuckles, shaking her head at us. "She is."

86

I narrow my eyes at Gabi. "Why aren't you drunk?" I ask her, noting how she's not acting crazy or loud, like Rosie is right now.

She shrugs with a smirk. "Maybe because I have a higher tolerance than a toddler?" she offers, tugging on my hand. "Now come on. You guys have rested enough. This is my bachelorette party."

I lift off the booth with a sigh, and roll my eyes. "Lord help me."

"You're being so dramatic," Gabi replies, arching a brow. "Dancing is fun."

I tilt my head. "Not when I'm pregnant, and tired, and a single cough makes me pee."

Gabi shivers in disgust, screwing her face up. "Definitely too much information. But regardless, I'm not letting you sit in that booth all night long. It's my bachelorette party. We need to have some fun."

I let out a laugh when she tugs my hand, and follow behind, but I freeze, when I feel something I haven't done in a long time. "Gabi—"

Gabi notices I'm not moving, and glances behind her shoulder, shaking her head. "I'm not letting you make any excuses. Let's go."

"Gabi, I really—"

"Uh uh," she says. "We're going to dance, and you're going to love it, and that's the end of it."

"*Gabi!*"

She turns around at my raised voice, and her brows dip as she searches my eyes. "What?" she asks, concern etched on her face. "What's wrong?"

I shake my head, glancing down at the wet patch on my pants, and Gabi's eyes follow, widening at the sight.

Madi sucks in a breath. "Is that …"

I nod, feeling the trickle down my legs. "I think my water just broke."

Chapter 12

AIDEN

Holy shit.

Holy fucking shit.

"This is not happening. There is no way this is fucking happening right now," I mutter to myself, my body shaking as I try to push past the mass amount of people standing in my way.

"You need to calm down," Grayson says beside me, placing his hand on my shoulder. "Rosie says the girls took her to the hospital. Everything's fine."

I shake my head, unable to make my lungs open up and breathe. I feel like I'm suffocating, and I want out. "I can't," I say, swallowing down the large rock sized knot in my throat as I glance at the people blocking the exit. "I can't fucking calm down. My wife is having my baby. Right fucking now." *Jesus.* The words coming out of my mouth make the situation ten times more real, and I can't fucking breathe again.

I can't even imagine how Leila is feeling right now. She was supposed to be having some fun with the girls tonight, but instead she's in fucking labor.

And I'm not there.

"Get the fuck out of my way," I yell, shoving past everyone in front of me, not giving a shit what anyone thinks. The only thing that matters is getting to the hospital.

I should have fucking left when I wanted to. The guys were all drunk, and I was clearly winning the game of poker, and all I wanted was to get out and see Leila. If I had listened to my gut, I'd be with her right now, and this wouldn't be happening. I'd be with her when her water broke. I'd be with her when we got a cab and headed to the hospital. I would have fucking *been* with her.

"Hey, what the fu—Aiden Pierce?" I turn my head to the side, seeing a group of guys looking like they're in their early twenties with their eyes on me. The one in front narrows his eyes as he sizes me up, but then they widen when he realizes it's me. "Holy shit. It is you. Yo, man, can we get a picture? I'm a huge fan."

I shake my head before I can even think about it. "I'm sorry, not today," I tell them, barely casting them a glance before I push through the crowd again. Any other day I would have stopped to talk to them, maybe take a picture or sign their shoes or something. But nothing in this world is going to stop me from getting to Leila right now. No matter what I have to do.

"Aiden." I turn around at the sound of Lucas's distinct voice, and see him gesturing to the corner of the club which is pretty empty, joined by Chris who looks like he's about to pass out. I don't think he's been this drunk in a long time, and I kinda feel bad that his bachelor party ended abruptly, but then again, I'm about to meet my baby. "There's another exit over here."

"Thank fuck," I mutter under my breath, turning around to head toward him. Grayson follows behind, and we push through the back doors, the cold air hitting our skins as soon as were out of the club.

"I've called a cab," Grayson says, pocketing his phone a second later. I blow out a breath. This is the worst thing right here. Waiting. Standing around with nothing to do but think, and worry, and think some more. "Are you okay, man?"

I shake my head, words jumbled up in my brain, my heart beating a million miles per hour, and sweat dripping down my back. "I can't believe Leila is having the baby right now."

"She just went into labor," Lucas says, reassuringly. "She won't be having the baby right this minute. You still have time."

I blow out a heavy breath, hoping he's right, but at the same time, my mind won't stop overthinking. "You don't know that," I say, feeling my chest ache. I just want to be with my girl right now.

"Hey, calm down," Grayson murmurs. "It's going to be okay. Leila's strong."

I know. She's the strongest woman I know. The best woman I know. The best mother I know. And… damn it. I should be there. "I just… the baby was supposed to be here in three weeks. We still had three weeks left to prepare."

"These things happen," Chris slurs, slowly sobering up as he pats me on the back. "But there's nothing to worry about. You're ready man. You're a great dad."

I almost laugh, seeing him drunk as he tries to help me, but then the cab pulls up, and panic settles in once again. I don't waste time, opening the doors and sliding in the black cab, the guys joining me before it drives off.

"I'll give you a hundred if you speed," I tell the driver, whom doesn't think twice before pressing his foot down on the gas, speeding through the traffic.

"We're here," the driver murmurs a few minutes later, which makes me breathe again.

I don't even know how long it takes for me to get out of the cab, and rush inside those hospital doors, but it can't be more than a minute. And by the time I reach the front desk, I'm out of breath, and unable to speak properly.

"Wife," I pant, trying to catch my breath. "Baby."

The woman at the desk widens her eyes, and her lips part as she takes me in. "Aiden Pierce?" she asks, seemingly shocked.

"I don't have time for this," I say, leaning on the desk. "My wife is having a baby right now. Where the hell is she?"

Her brows furrow, clearly confused on who my wife is, which... *come the fuck on*. She's the hottest model ever to walk this earth, she glances down at her monitor screen, and clicks about a thousand times before she asks, "Name?"

"Leila Pierce."

Another million fucking clicks, and then she lifts her head. "She's in room ten."

My shoulders slump, and I turn around, heading into the elevator, the guys following behind.

As soon as the ding goes off, and the doors open, I run out of the elevator, down the corridor, when I see Gabi blowing into a paper bag. My heart immediately starts to pound in my chest. "What's wrong? Is Leila okay?" I ask.

She nods, pulling the paper bag away from her face. "She's fine. I'm just…" She shakes her head, and waves her arms. "Just go, she's in there."

Chris reaches Gabi, lifting her chin to make her look at him, and I turn around, pushing open the doors until I see my girl on the bed, her hair tied up in a messy bun as she rests her arm on her forehead.

My body immediately calms and I blow out the biggest breath. "Baby," I murmur, smiling when I see her eyes lock with mine.

Her eyes widen and she reaches out for me. I grab her hand and sit on the chair beside the bed. Rosie and Madi leave the room, and I lift Leila's hand, pressing my lips against her knuckles. "I tried to get here earlier. There were so many people in my fucking way, and then the cab took forever and…" I squeeze my eyes closed, placing her palm against my cheek.

"You're here now," she says, her voice sweet, and calm. "That's all that matters."

I chuckle a little, eyeing her subdued state. "The drugs doing their job?" I ask.

She nods, a soft hum leaving her lips. "That baby's coming."

"I know, gorgeous."

"Are you ready?" she asks, her sweet green eyes blinking up at me.

I let out a laugh. "You're the one going through labor, baby. I should be asking you that. How are you feeling?"

She sighs. "The drugs mellowed me out."

"I can see that," I murmur, brushing the stray strands of hair out of her face, feeling the sweat build up on her forehead. I lean down to press my lips against hers, my body warming at the feel of her. "You're doing so fucking good, baby."

She twists her head to face me, slightly narrowing her eyes. "I'm not even doing anything yet."

I shake my head. She doesn't realize how wrong she is. "You've been carrying our baby for nine months. That's a hell of a lot of work. You've made an amazing home in there, and now, you're about to deliver our baby."

Her green eyes soften when she looks at me, and my heart beats so fucking loudly with the love I have for this woman right here. "I love you," she says with a sigh.

"I love you," I tell her, staring into her eyes as her hand squeezes in mine. "I'm grateful every day for that spin the bottle game back in college or else I would have never known what true happiness would be like."

The door opens, and I turn my head to see a woman walking in, smiling at us. "Hi, you must be the dad," she says, glancing down at the medical sheet before she lifts her head. "You guys ready to have a baby?"

I swallow harshly. "Wait. She's having the baby right now?" I ask, my eyes widening, unable to make sense of it. I thought it'd be maybe an hour or two before she was ready to push but fuck, it's happening right now. And I'm so glad I got here in time.

"Yep," she replies, pulling on her gloves before she reaches under my wife's gown. "She's at ten centimeters, it's time to start pushing."

"Holy shit," I murmur, turning back to Leila. "You've got this, gorgeous."

She stares into my eyes, and squeezes my hand as the doctor puts her in position, ready to push.

The next hour and a half go by in a quick blur. Groans, screams and so much sweat, until the world unblurs and I hear the sound of a baby crying.

"Holy fuck," I murmur, glancing at the doctor as she picks up my baby, and Leila lies her head back on the pillow, blowing out a much-needed breath. "You did it," I say, tears streaming down my cheeks as I reach down and kiss Leila, brushing the hair sticking to her forehead away. "You fucking did it, baby."

"Congratulations," the OBGYN says, as she walks toward us with our baby. "It's a girl."

My eyes widen, and a grin spreads across my face as she places our baby girl on Leila's chest. I smile down at my two girls, feeling like my life is complete. My heart feels like it's about to burst.

"Hi baby," Leila murmurs, lifting the baby's finger as she cries out in her mother's arms.

Leila lifts her head to meet my eyes. "It's a girl," she murmurs. I nod, unable to say anything, the feelings inside me too fucking much, and Leila's lips twist into a smirk. "Can I tell you a secret?"

"Of course, baby," I say, cupping her face in my hand.

"I was secretly hoping it was a girl, too," she whispers which makes me chuckle.

"You were?"

She nods, glancing down at our baby for a second before she meets my eyes again. "I want you to be happy, and I know you really wanted a girl."

My brows dip, and I shuffle closer to her on the bed, shaking my head. "Leila, *you* make me happy. You always make me happy, baby, and I might have joked around about wanting another girl, but I would have loved this baby so fucking much even if it was a boy."

She smiles, and then lets out a sigh. "We always have next time."

I let out a laugh, nodding in agreement. I can't wait to grow our family. "Deal," I say. "But only after a very, very long break." We waited three years before having another, and I think the time we spent with just Nova was perfect. I want to get to know my daughters before we decide to bring another baby into the mix. And besides, Leila needs a break. Raising two toddlers will be hard enough.

"Deal," she murmurs, smiling down at our baby. "She looks just like you," my girl whispers, both of our eyes locked on our sweet baby in her mother's arms.

I let out a scoff. "I love her, but she kind of looks like an alien right now." I arch a brow. "Should I take offense to that?"

Leila rolls her eyes, letting out a laugh. "She has your gorgeous blue eyes," she says with a sweet smile that makes my heart thud against my chest.

Fuck. I love this woman. Every day, I wake up and think I can't possibly love her more than I already do. And every day, I'm proven wrong.

I pick up my daughter's tiny little fingers, which immediately wrap around my pointer finger. "What do you want to call her?" I ask my wife.

"I named the last one," she says. "It's your turn now."

I steal a glance at Leila, my brows dipping. "Are you sure? You did the hard part, baby. You should get to name her."

She shakes her head. "You can name her. If it's horrendous, then I can always veto."

A laugh bubbles out of me, and my eyes drift to my daughter, seeing her eyes closed shut, her pink, pouty lips pressed against her mother's skin, her dark, brown hair matching Leila's.

"Talia," I murmur, the name feeling right as I look at my daughter.

"Talia," Leila repeats to herself, her lips curling into a smile. "I love it."

"Yeah?"

My wife glances at our daughter, holding her in her arms. "Hi, Talia Pierce," she whispers to the baby. "Welcome to the world. I'm your mommy."

"And I'm your daddy," I say. "And I can't wait to spoil you rotten."

"Can we come in now?" I hear Gabi's voice, from the other side of the door, and we let out a laugh and Leila nods.

I gently lift Talia into my arms, and hold her hand in my hand. She's so tiny, so precious, so beautiful. "Come in," I tell them, because I have no doubt the rest of the guys are all behind that door.

The door opens, and they all walk inside, their eyes searching for the baby until they see her in my arms.

"Guys, meet Talia Pierce," I whisper, letting them see my gorgeous daughter.

Madeline brings a hand to her mouth as her eyes well up with tears. "She's so beautiful," she whispers back, her voice growing wobbly. Lucas wraps his arms around Madi, pressing a kiss to the side of her head.

"Why is she blue?" Gabi murmurs, her mouth half full, and I furrow my brows down at her.

"Are you... are you eating a sandwich?"

Chris lets out a laugh, now completely sober. "It's her second."

"I don't know how you can eat at a time like this," Grayson says, brushing his hair back.

Gabi shoots him a glare, swallowing down her bite. "I eat when I'm nervous, alright?"

"Why are you nervous?" Grayson asks her. "You didn't have a baby."

She shrugs. "Just am. Get off my dick, *jeez*," she says with an eye roll before taking another bite.

"I'm sorry we stole your thunder," Leila tells Gabi, looking apologetic. "She was supposed to come in three weeks."

"Blame the baby," I say, shaking my head. "Not me."

"Aiden," Leila chastises.

I turn to my wife, giving her a look. "Have you seen Gabi's right hook? I'm not getting hit with that."

Gabi swallows, shaking her head, and reaches out to lift Talia's finger. "Are you kidding? For this girl you can steal the whole damn sky."

I smile down at Leila who returns my smile, and I know without a doubt, this is what I was put on this planet for. This was what I was made for, and I'm the luckiest guy in the world that my gorgeous wife even spared a second glance at me.

And I'll make sure to show her just how grateful I am every day of my life.

The Call

Chapter 13

LUCAS

"Look how tiny she is."

Turning my head to my right, my lips curl into a smile at the sight of Aiden grinning down at his baby daughter in the maternity ward through the glass. I swear he almost shoves his face against the glass, trying to get as close as he possibly can.

But I can't help but feel a twinge of sadness in my heart, knowing that Madeline and I will probably never be in this position.

"Surprising since, you know… you're a giant and all," Grayson says with a scoff. "But seeing how tall Nova is at her age, I don't doubt that this one will be just as tall."

Aiden chuckles a little, and then returns right back to staring at his daughter in a pool of other babies. "Fuck," he whispers, shaking his head. "This feels …"

"I can imagine," Grayson says. "I mean she's not even my kid, and I still feel like…" He trails off, letting out a hard breath.

Aiden nudges him on the shoulder, looking down at his best friend. "Hurry up and make a baby so you and Rosie can feel what I feel," he says with a grin. "It's amazing man."

James makes a noise, and wraps his arms around his husband. "Well, I'm checked out of this conversation," he says before they both walk away.

I let out a laugh. My best friend has never once liked kids. Even when he was one. So, his and Carter's decision of not having any of their own didn't shock me one bit.

"Patience," Grayson says. "We haven't even gotten married yet. I want my girl wearing my ring when we have a baby," he says with a smile on his face. Seems like the only time Grayson smiles is when he's with Rosie. Or talking about Rosie. Or thinking about Rosie. Other than that, I can't say I've seen him smile for anything else.

"Fine," Aiden says with a sigh. "I just want you guys to know what being a dad feels like." His eyes turn to his daughter and he shakes his head. "Fuck. I can't believe I'm a dad again."

"Again?" Grayson asks with a scoff. "I didn't realize you stopped being a dad."

"You know what I mean," Aiden replies with an eye roll. "It's going to be different with a baby. I'm so used to Nova being able to talk, and walk. This is going to be a whole new ball game for me again."

"Has Nova met her sister yet?" I ask.

He shakes his head. "No, not yet. We Facetimed Leila's parents, but we wanted Nova to meet Talia in person." His grin widens. "She hasn't stopped talking about the baby since she found out," he says. "She even rearranged her room to make space for the baby." A laugh bubbles out of him. "I don't want to break her heart when I tell her the baby will have her own room."

"Two kids man," Chris murmurs, shaking his head. "That will be crazy."

Aiden shrugs. "We'll make it work," he says. "Thank fuck the season is over so I can stay home with my girls for a while."

"Jesus, I didn't even think of the fact you'll have three girls in the house now," Grayson replies with widened eyes.

Aiden though, doesn't seem at all bothered by it as he laughs. "It might sound daunting but I know I'll fucking love it. And you never know, maybe in the future we'll have a little boy running around," he says, which makes my brows shoot up.

"This one just popped out, and you're already planning the next?"

"Leila was the one who actually mentioned it," he tells me with a laugh. "But I told her it would be a while before we even think of having another baby."

Grayson lets out an unconvinced scoff. "Good luck with that," he says with an arched brow.

Aiden flips him off, and takes a step back from the glass. "Speaking of, I'm going to go and see my beautiful wife," he says with a grin. "See you guys."

When Aiden walks into the hospital room, the door opens a second later and Gabi rushes out, heading toward the bathroom. Chris furrows his brows, and follows behind her. Rosie walks out of the room, walking toward Grayson, and they both turn to face the maternity ward, glancing at the babies and chuckling to themselves as they look at each other lovingly.

Mark my words, those two will be the next to have kids.

The door opens again, and I glance back to see Madi pushing through the door, her eyes meeting mine when she lifts her head. My heart pounds against my chest the second I see her. She's so fucking beautiful, even after spending the night in the hospital. Her lips lift into a smile as she joins me, and I don't waste any time, cupping her face before I lean down and press my lips against hers.

"What have you been doing out here?" she asks, glancing behind me at the maternity ward, and I notice as her smile slips, a saddened look replacing it as she looks at the babies in there.

My heart hurts at the possibility of never being able to have a kid, but mostly because of *her*. I see how much Madeline wants a baby. She wants to be a mom, and she'd be a hell of a good one, and it kills me that it hasn't happened for her.

"It's going to be okay," I reassure her, as I press a kiss against the side of her head.

"I know," she whispers, unconvincingly.

I can't blame her for not believing me. We've been trying for years. Years, we've spent having appointments with countless of doctors, trying to make a baby.

Months, we've been waiting to hear back from the adoption agency, and still, not a single word.

When making a baby naturally wasn't working, the other natural option was adoption. Madeline was adopted when she was a baby, and she adores her family. So, the thought of being that for someone, of giving a child a loving home, was the easiest decision in the world.

But what hasn't been easy, is the process. Waiting, and waiting, and *waiting* for someone to call and let us know there's a baby available for us to adopt has been so hard, and disheartening, and I can tell it's taking a toll on Madi.

"Are you sure you don't want to tell our friends?" I ask her. The only people we've told is our family, and even that was hard. No one else knows how hard it's been for us to have kids, or how we've decided to adopt, or how we haven't heard back from anyone yet. "It might be easier to talk to the girls about it," I suggest.

Madi shakes her head, ripping her eyes away from the babies to look up at me with glassy eyes. "No," she says, determined. "I don't want to give them false hope in case we…" She presses her lips together, unable to voice the possibility of us never getting the call. "This will never be us," she says, gesturing to the glass. "You'll never get to stand here and look out there and see your baby."

My brows dip, my chest aching at the sight of tears in her eyes. "You never know," I tell her. "It could happen, Madeline. And if it doesn't, it doesn't mean we can never have a family." I clutch her face in my hand, smoothing my thumb over her soft cheek. "We'll get that call, Madi. You'll be a mom. I'll be a dad."

She drops her eyes, the subtle shake of her head breaking my heart, but not as much as her next words do. "You can always leave, you know?"

My brows furrow, and I lift her chin with my thumb, making her look at me. "What the hell are you talking about?"

Her lips part, and her glassy eyes look right at me when she says, "I wouldn't blame you if you wanted to leave. I know how much you want a baby. You could find another woman that can give you what I can't and—"

"Stop," I blurt out, anger building inside me. "Don't you ever say those words again." My heart drops to my stomach at the reminder. "I want a baby, of course I do. But not more than I want you." Her eyes well up with tears. "There is nothing in this world that could ever make me walk away from you. Madeline, I haven't even spared a glance at another woman since the second you walked into my life. How could you ever think I would ever walk away from you?" I ask, bewildered at the fact she ever uttered those words. "This doesn't change anything about the way I feel about you. I love *you*, princesa. I want a family with *you*. No one else. You."

"Lucas," she whispers, her voice wobbly and unstable.

"You can tell me you don't want kids, and it wouldn't change anything for me. All I've ever wanted was you, and that will never change. But if you tell me you want kids, then we can keep trying, or look into a surrogate, or wait for the adoption agency to call. But all I want is a family with you. With kids, or without kids. I'll be the happiest fucking guy as long as I'm with you."

"You really mean that?" she asks, glancing up at me with hope swimming in her eyes.

"I really do," I say, pressing my forehead against hers. "It kills me that I haven't been able to give you a baby yet, but we can keep trying," I tell her, pulling back with a grin. "It's pretty fun."

She lets out a laugh, shoving me in the chest, and I know, everything will be okay.

Her smile settles, and her eyes lock with mine. "I *want* to adopt," she breathes out, making my shoulders drop in relief.

These past few years, Madi hasn't let herself speak about what she wants. I think that's a big part of why she hasn't told the girls yet. She doesn't want to put the idea out there in case it gets snatched up from her.

But even when we were first discussing adoption, she wouldn't let herself say what she wanted. So finally hearing her admit she wants this, that she wants to adopt a baby feels like a weight off my chest.

"Then we'll adopt," I tell her, loving the idea. "I can't wait to give a child a loving home. Just like your parents did with you," I say, tucking a strand of hair behind her ear. "Look how great you turned out." I flash her a smile which she returns.

"It might not happen for a while, though," she says, her smile slipping. "Are you okay with that?"

I nod, reaching for her hand, before I lift it and press my lips against her knuckles. "I'll wait for as long as it takes, *princesa*."

Her eyes soften, lovingly, and I lean down ready to kiss my stunning wife, but our attention is snagged by the sound of Gabi's voice.

"Come on," she says, making Madi and I turn out heads, seeing Gabi and Chris running toward a storage closet, the door closing behind them a second later.

I arch a brow. "Are they going to fuck in a hospital?" I ask with a laugh, already knowing the answer.

"It's Gabi and Chris," Madi replies with a chuckle. "Of course they are."

Chapter 14

When the phone dings with a new text for the hundredth time today, Lucas lets out a deep groan, rolling over to face me. "Please don't tell me that's who I think it is," he says, arching a brow as he buries his head in the pillow.

Today has been a long ass day. From rushing Leila to the hospital last night, to staying at the hospital with the rest of the guys the whole day, I'm exhausted, and so is Lucas by the look on his face.

Fixing the silk wrap on my head, I flash him a smirk, shuffling down on the bed to lie on my side, facing him. "It's the twenty-first text I've gotten from her today alone," I say with a chuckle.

He lets out another groan, and reaches an arm around my waist, tugging until I'm plastered against him. His lips land on my collarbone, pressing featherlight kisses on my skin. "I don't know what you expected when you agreed to be Gabi's maid of honor," he gruffs out, between kisses.

When he lifts his head, and his eyes meet mine, my chest starts knocking against my chest in a pattern I'm all too familiar with. I'm still so in love with this man, and he's as handsome as ever, and I'm the luckiest girl in the world to be able to cuddle up to him at night, and wake up to him in the morning.

Which is why the quick blip in my chest makes my smile slip. He's so amazing. So kind, and gracious and treats me like a queen. I know he'd be an amazing dad, and I hate that I can't give him that. I try really fucking hard not to let it eat me alive, but today was just one of those days where the overthinking got the better of me.

Seeing Leila have her second baby, and seeing the look on Aiden's face made my stomach drop. I'm so happy for them, they deserve the best in this world. But I couldn't help but imagine how Lucas must have been feeling while seeing one of his best friends have another baby, while we'd been trying for years, and… nothing.

And then when I saw him standing by the maternity ward, looking at the babies, I just… broke.

I forced the words out of my throat, giving him a way out, a way to become a father with someone else, but merely saying the words was like my throat was being sliced into a million pieces. The thought of him moving on with someone else, and starting a family with them… it would have killed me.

I hated the thought, and while I wanted him to be happy, I wanted him to be happy with me. I was really relieved when my amazing husband made sure to reassure me that he wouldn't even entertain the idea.

"I offered to be her maid of honor," I remind him, my breath coming out a little harder as he kisses my skin, a low groan escaping his throat. "Besides, Leila's wedding turned out amazing. I'm really good at organizing."

He chuckles against my skin, lifting his head to glance at me with a smirk. "Mmm. I love when you talk dirty."

I let out a laugh, and Lucas dips down again, leaving open mouth kisses on my jaw, when the phone dings again.

Lucas groans, his voice vibrating against my skin, and he buries his head in my chest. "Only one more day to get through," he murmurs.

"And then they're finally off to their honeymoon," I reply, my fingers getting lost in his curly brown hair.

Lucas lifts his head, blinking up at me. "And maybe we can have ours, too," he says, which makes my brows furrow.

"We already had our honeymoon."

He nods, his lips lifting into a smile as his big hands curl around my waist. "How about we take another one?"

My frown deepens, confusion taking over my face. "You want to marry me again?" I ask.

He chuckles. "I'd marry you over and over again If I could, but that's not exactly what I was thinking." When I arch a brow, he clutches my face in his hands. "I was thinking we could take a little vacation. Have some time for ourselves."

My eyes widen a little, loving the idea, but… "Why?"

"Why not?" he asks with a shrug. "We both work hard as fuck, and the house is almost done," he says which makes me smile at the reminder. When Lucas first told me he was building me a house, I didn't quite believe him. But lo and behold, he designed everything, just how I wanted it. He came up with the blueprints, and even placed the first brick. "Why not take a little vacation before there's a baby?"

My brows knit together. "Do you know something I don't?"

He laughs, shaking his head. "Mads, it will happen," he says with a certainty I want to believe in. "I know it will. I can feel it in my bones."

My breath hitches. I love how certain he is. I love how excited he is about this. A lot of people think of adoption as the last option, but Lucas seems like he really wants this. "Do you ever feel sad that you won't have a baby of your own?" I ask him.

He tilts his head. "It will be mine."

"You know what I mean," I say pointedly.

He shrugs. "No," he says without hesitation. "I don't care that the baby won't share my DNA. Don't get me wrong, I would have loved to see a baby with a little mix of us both," he says, smirking as he traces his thumb over my bottom lip. "I just know it would be so fucking cute, but am I sad about giving a child a home?" He shakes his head. "Definitely not."

When we told our family about our choice to adopt, I asked my parents about their decision to adopt me. They couldn't have kids after Nia, and I always wondered how they felt about that, but they told me it was the best decision they ever made, and that they never once questioned it. It made me even more excited for the process.

"I want to be someone's mother," I murmur, glancing up at Lucas. I haven't let myself admit it. A part of me thought if I didn't say what I truly wanted, then it couldn't be taken away from me. But I do want it. I want it so much.

Lucas smiles, leaning down to kiss me. "And you will be," he says, pressing another kiss to my lips. "You're so brave. And beautiful. And goddamn, I'm so fucking lucky we got stuck in that elevator all those years ago," he says, pulling back to look into my eyes. "I'm the luckiest motherfucker ever."

"Because I'm rich?" I tease with a smirk.

He chuckles, settling on top of me, and arches a brow at me. "Baby, we're both rich," he replies, making me roll my eyes. "But it's definitely not because of that." He curls his hand around my neck, lifting my head. "I'm lucky because every single morning I get to wake up, roll over and see this face." His thumb caresses my cheek, his eyes scanning my features. "And touch this body," he murmurs while his other hand slowly traces my stomach, lifting the material of my silk pajamas up slowly, slowly, until his thumb swipes over my hard nipple, eliciting a moan out of me. "And feel this pussy."

A loud moan rips from my throat when his other hand leaves my face, and slides down my body, sneaking into my pajama shorts, before he swipes his middle finger between my pussy. "Lucas," I gasp when he thrusts his finger inside.

He grunts, curling his finger to hit a spot deep inside of me that makes me buck into him. "That's right, baby. Let everyone in this hotel know who takes care of you." He pulls back his finger, and I almost groan in impatience before he thrusts two fingers back inside of me, earning another breathless moan from me. "These gorgeous tits," he says, cupping my breast. "These long fucking legs." His eyes devour me, darkening at the sight of my body exposed for him, his hands all over me. "Goddamn. You get hotter every year."

"So do you," I gasp, lifting my hand to touch his face. "I love your beard."

He groans, a smirk pulling at the corner of his lips. "I bet you'd like it even more scratching the inside of your thighs."

He quickly pulls the sheets off us, and his eyes scream hunger as he pulls off my pajama top, and shorts, baring me to him. Lucas doesn't waste any time before he kneels at the foot of the bed, and spreads my legs wide open, placing my left foot over his shoulder.

His lips first press against my inner thigh, teasing me, making me lose my mind as he leaves open mouth kisses so close to where I want him. But when the first swipe of his tongue hits me, I let out a guttural moan, my clit vibrating to life.

"God yes," I gasp out, the pleasure blinding me. I can't believe there was a time when I thought I didn't like this.

He groans against my pussy, his beard tickling the inside of my thighs as he licks and French kisses my clit, sucking it into his mouth. "Your noises drive me fucking wild, Mads," he grunts against me, slowly flicking his tongue over my clit, which makes my legs shake.

"You make me feel so good," I moan, squeezing my eyes closed as I let myself feel. The sound of wet sloppy kisses on my pussy makes me clench around nothing as he continues his torturous licks.

"That's because I know my girl," he murmurs, sucking me into his mouth. "I know every single inch of you. I know that

114

when I do this," he says, thrusting a finger inside me, which makes my hips buck up into him. "You buck your hips like you're searching for my cock. And when I do this," he murmurs right before wrapping his lips around my clit and gives it a hard suck. "You'll moan like crazy." And sure enough, I let out a loud moan, my fingers tangling in his hair.

"Fuck me, Lucas," I plead, wanting him inside me right now.

He lifts between my legs, and my eyes snap open in time to see him grin down at me, his beard dripping wet. "You don't even have to ask, baby." He shuffles on the bed, until I feel his cock tapping against my entrance, slowly rubbing between my pussy before he thrusts it inside.

I grip onto his arms, needing support as he breaches me, his thick cock hitting a spot that makes me see stars.

"Holy fuck, Madi," he grunts. "You're gripping me so tight... *fuck*. Let me look at you, baby." He leans back, slowly pushing his cock into me as his eyes zone in on where we're connected, a low groan escaping him.

I don't even have time to think before he grips my waist, and flips me over, placing me on my hands and knees. My heart lurches in my throat. Fuck yes. As much as I love looking at him when we have sex, this position makes him go deeper until I can practically feel him in my guts.

"I love you, *princesa*," he murmurs, his voice thick as he grips my waist, and pulls me into him, his cock rubbing against the crease of my ass. "Make sure you remember that, because it's going to feel like I don't."

A shiver runs up my spine as he rubs his cock against my wet pussy before he pushes his cock inside me in one hard, quick thrust.

My head drops to the bed as he fills me up, not even waiting for me to adjust before he pulls out and thrusts back in. Moans are ripped from my throat as he grabs my hips, and pulls me back against him, going as deep and hard as possible.

"Such a cute princess when we're in public," he grunts, lifting me so my back is plastered against his chest. "But when we're in private, you love my cock deep inside of you, don't you."

My only response is an agonized moan, my eyes squeezing hard as the pleasure rolls through me.

"Lucas," I gasp when his cock tunnels into me, hitting my g-spot. "I'm... fuck."

"That's it, baby. I can feel you," he grunts, tugging my earlobe between his teeth. "Come, baby. Come on my cock. Let me feel you drench me."

That's all it takes for my core to tighten up, and the orgasm to crash into me so hard I swear I almost black out. Moan after moan leaves my lips as Lucas keeps thrusting into me, my pussy squeezing around him.

"Fuck. You're so fucking wet, and tight. God damn Mads." He grunts, thrusting his cock into me until he groans in my ear, and I feel his thick, hot cum shoot inside me.

Lucas drops beside me, and curls a hand around my neck, pulling me into him so he can kiss me. I get lost in his kiss, clinging to him out of pure need.

I can't help but think of all the times we've done this with the purpose of having a baby. But this time, it's out of love, out of passion. And I'm determined not to let my mind think about whether if this time will be it. If this is the time we finally make a baby.

I don't think I care anymore. If it does happen, then that will be amazing. But if not, I know that Lucas and I won't stop until we have a family of our own.

And I'm so excited for that day.

Chapter 15

"You know there are more available seats in this bar, don't you?" James asks with a chuckle, arching a brow at my girl sat on my lap.

I shoot him a glare, pressing my lips together. *I know damn well there are*. I wrap an arm around Madi's waist, and pull her back, plastering her back against my chest.

Grayson snickers, taking a sip of his beer. "He's scared Gabi will pull her away again," he jokes.

Gabi tilts her head at us, furrowing her brows. "I'm not that bad, am I?"

Everyone else murmurs, looking distracted, and her brows shoot up at everyone avoiding her question. We're all walking on eggshells around her, since it's her wedding and all, but I let out a chuckle at her expression, and decide to tell her the truth.

"You kind of are," I tell her, seeing her brows knit together. Fuck. This is why no one else wanted to tell her. She gets this sad puppy look in her eyes, and no one wants her to be upset on the night before her wedding.

"Really?" she asks, looking to Madi for confirmation.

"It's okay," my amazing wife says, reassuring her best friend. "It's your wedding, and you want it to be perfect." She lifts her shoulder. "I get that. We all get that. I knew what I was signing up for when I accepted to be your maid of honor."

Gabi visibly relaxes, her lips lifting into a smile, but then her brows knit together. "But you're a hundred percent everything is ready to go for tomorrow, right?"

Madeline lets out a laugh, and nods. "Yes," she confirms. "The flowers are scheduled to arrive tomorrow at six. The cake will be there at ten, and the guests are arriving at nine." She tilts her head, flashing her a warm smile. "Everything will be perfect, Gabi. There's nothing to worry about."

Gabi sighs. "I guess."

Chris reaches for her hand, which makes her turn her eyes on him. "You should be excited, pretty girl. Not stressed," he says, but then his smile slips a little. "Are you not excited?"

Gabi shakes her head, clutching his face in her hand, and leans down to press a reassuring kiss on his lips. "Of course, I'm excited. I just want our wedding to be perfect. I want everything to go right." Chris returns her smile, and I swear my heart knocks in my chest at the sight of those two. They're so fucking perfect for each other. "I can't wait to be Mrs. Hudson," she tells him with a grin.

Chris chuckles. "Or I can be Mr. Miller?"

Gabi's brows lift. "You want to take my last name?" she asks him.

His shoulders lift in a shrug as his smile widens. "We could say 'we're the Millers'."

"Dude, that's so cool," Grayson says, smacking him on his arm. "I say take the cooler last name."

Chris laughs, but then turns his attention to Gabi, his expression settling. "Besides, it's my father's last name," he says. "I wouldn't be mad over losing that association to him. So, if you want me to change it to yours, then I'm in."

"Mine is also my father's," Gabi points out with a laugh. "How unfortunate that we both have assholes for dads."

Chris clutches her face in his hand, running his thumb over her cheek, Gabi's eyes meeting his. "We should make a whole new last name for us."

Gabi's eyes widen. "We could so something cool, like …"

"Parker," they both say in unison, their smiles widening. Those two have always been crazy about spiderman. It's no wonder they'd both choose that particular last name.

"You guys are not inventing a new last name," Grayson says with a grunt.

"Mind your business, Grayson," Gabi replies, keeping her eyes on Chris.

"You could name your son Peter," James adds with a wink. "That would be cool."

Gabi grunts, shaking her head. "Okay, no. That's too far. We're not a shitty spin off show," she says with an eye roll. "I think we should flip a coin and let fate decide."

Chris leans in and presses his lips to hers in a soft kiss, that luckily, ends quickly. I love those guys, but I've witnessed their make out sessions one too many times. "I love that idea," he says with stars in his eyes.

"Fuck. We're getting old," James says with a huff. "Getting married, having kids." He grunts, shaking his head. "How do you guys think Aiden and Leila are doing?" he asks.

"They're doing amazing," Rosie says. "Leila's texting me hourly updates, and turns out, Aiden can rock Talia to sleep in under a minute."

"Figures," Grayson says with a scoff. "That guy is good at everything he does."

"I bet that pisses Leila off," Gabi says with a snicker. "I can just imagine the baby crying for hours, and then Aiden comes in, and it knocks out immediately. I'd pay to see that."

"It?" Rosie asks with a raised brow.

Gabi rolls her eyes. "She," she says, waving a hand. "You know what I mean."

"When are you guys going to be next?" Grayson asks, looking at us with a smile, which makes Madi freeze on my lap. "I want to see a little baby Silva."

Fuck.

Madi shifts on my lap, and I tighten my hold on her waist, knowing the feelings going through her right now. "I uh…" Her voice cracks a little and it breaks my fucking heart. "I don't know." She lifts off my lap, smoothing her dress down, and grabs her purse from the seat beside me. "I need to go to the bathroom. Excuse me."

I watch, my heart in my throat, as my wife rushes into the bathroom, without a doubt about to cry.

"OW. What the fuck was that for?"

I turn my head, seeing Grayson clutch his arm, scowling at James, who's scowling back.

"Don't fucking bring kids up in front of them anymore," James says which makes my pulse race.

Fuck. Madi doesn't want to tell anyone, and while James knows, since he's family, no one else does, and I really don't want them to find out like this.

I shoot James a look that tells him to quit it. While I appreciate my best friend for sticking up for me, and Mads, it's also bringing some suspicion I'd rather not deal with right now.

"Okay fuck," Grayson says, his eyes widening as he glances at me, regret in his eyes. "I didn't know that you guys didn't like it. Do you guys not want kids or—"

"It's not that," I interrupt, shaking my head. Fuck, I can't do this. I lift myself off the chair, gesturing behind me with my thumb. "I'm going to go check on her."

I turn around, and head toward the women's bathroom, knocking before I enter. The place is pretty empty so I doubt there would be any other women in here, and right now, I need to check on my wife.

The door opens with a creak, and I see Madi gripping the sink, her head bowed as soft cries leave her lips. Fuck. This feels like my heart is being ripped out of my chest.

"Baby." I rush toward her, quickly wrapping my arms around her as she cries against my chest. "It's okay," I tell her, my eyes filling up with tears. "I know it's fucking hard to hear that."

She shakes her head against me, sniffling as the crying settles, and lifts her head to look up at me. "Maybe we should tell them," she says with a sniffle. "If they know about our… situation, then they'll finally stop asking." She lets out a deep breath, closing her eyes. "I just don't want them to be disappointed."

I lift her chin with my thumb. "They would never be disappointed, Mads," I reassure her. "They're just curious, *princesa*. They see how amazing we are, and how much we love each other, and they're just wondering when we'll finally be parents."

Her bottom lip trembles as she shakes her head. "But we won't."

"Yes, we will," I tell her, sliding a hand to clutch her face, needing to be near her. "We'll get the call, Madi. We'll have a family." Her eyes lock with mine, and I see the hope in them, wanting it to be true. "We'll wait to tell them until then. You were right. It's a lot of pressure, and more questions we both don't want to answer," I say with an arched brow, which she smiles at. "Besides, we should be looking at the silver lining in all of this."

She lifts a brow. "There's a silver lining in not being able to have kids?" she says, dryly.

"You know what the great thing about not having any kids right now is?" I ask her with a smirk.

She doesn't look convinced as she arches a brow. "What?"

"We don't have to leave early and take care of them," I say with a shrug. "We can stay out all." I lean in to kiss her lips. "Night." *Kiss.* "Long."

She chuckles as I press my lips against her jaw. "I guess you're right."

I hum against her skin, trailing my hands up her arms. "You know what else is great about not having kids right now?"

She shivers when my kisses become heavier, longer, harder, and sucks in a breath when I slip her straps off her shoulders. "What?" she says, breathlessly.

My lips twitch into a smirk as I slowly let my hands trace her gorgeous body, covered in a dark plum dress that clings to her body, making my mouth water. When my hands reach her thighs, I pause, keeping my eyes on hers, before I lift it up her soft thigh, and slip it inside her underwear, eliciting a beautiful gasp out of her glossy pink lips.

"I can do this," I say, running my middle finger between her folds. "And there's no one to stop us."

"Lucas," she pants, gripping onto my arm as her hips buck.

A groan escapes my throat when I feel how dripping wet my wife is. "Spread your legs wider," I tell her. "Make room for me, *princesa.*"

She does as she's told and spreads her legs until I slip a finger inside her, feeling her walls tighten around me. "That's it," I grunt, when she lets out a moan. "Fuck, you're drenched."

I want to taste her. I want to fall to my knees, lift up this pretty little dress, and eat her pussy until I'm satiated. But the thing about being in public is, we have to be quick. And I like to enjoy my dessert.

Another delicious moan leaves her lips and I lose my mind, diving in to capture her lips, swallowing every desperate noise she makes down. My girl is loud as fuck, which absolutely drives me crazy with need, but I don't want anyone to find us here, with my fingers deep in her pussy

Luckily, I know how to touch my wife until she writhes with pleasure, and in no time, she's bucking her hips, moaning, gripping my arm, squeezing her eyes closed until the orgasm hits her like a tsunami, and a flood of liquid surrounds my finger.

Fuck. As soon as I get home, I'm going to lick her clean. I pull back with a chuckle, adoring how flustered she is. "You see how fun that was?" I say with a smirk.

She lets out a laugh, leaning in to kiss me, but then the bathroom door is flung open, and we both break apart to see Gabi standing at the door.

My hand is still inside my girl, and it's very obvious as Gabi's eyes fall to it before she turns around and groans. "Come on," she says. "In a bathroom, really?"

"We couldn't wait," I say, Madi and I sharing a smirk.

"Your hotel is five-minutes away," she says, before letting out another groan. "Hurry up. I need to use the bathroom, and I don't want anyone in here."

We pull apart, and make ourselves decent, quickly washing up before we make our way out of the bathroom.

"Don't stay up all night fucking," Gabi yells back, the whole bar clearly hearing her. "I'm getting married tomorrow."

"We know," Madi and I say in unison, before the bathroom door closes.

Chapter 16

My head turns toward the bathroom door when I hear Lucas let out a whistle. He leans against the bathroom door, his arms crossed as he checks me out, giving me a once over. He whistles again which makes me roll my eyes, unable to stop the smile from spreading across my face as my husband devours me with his eyes.

He steps away from the door and heads toward me, placing his hands on my hips when he reaches me. "Holy shit, baby," he murmurs, moving my hair to the side so he can place a kiss on my neck. "You look so fucking good."

I let out a chuckle, turning back to face the mirror, loving how my husband is still crazy attracted to me after three years of being married.

"Are you sure you're not going to upstage Gabi in this dress?" he asks, smoothing his hands over my dress.

I lift my head, our eyes meeting in the mirror, and let out a scoff. "Trust me. There's no way anyone can upstage her. Her dress is so beautiful. Rosie spent a whole year making it for her," I tell him, looking at him over my shoulder. "And you know how expensive her dresses are."

It's crazy to think how far she's come since college. When I met her, she was innocent, and too good for this world. But now she's the CEO of her own designer firm. I couldn't be more proud for her.

Lucas makes a noise, trailing his lips against my shoulder. "I don't think I'm going to be able to tear my eyes off of you long enough to even glance at her dress," he says, which makes me chuckle before I turn around to face him.

My hands rest on the lapels of his tux, seeing his gorgeous face grinning down at me. "You look really good," I tell him.

His grin widens, and he lets out a soft laugh. "Yeah?"

"Mhmm," I confirm with a nod as I let my hands run over the fabric of his tux. "Really good," I emphasize, pulling my bottom lip between my teeth.

His low, raspy chuckle makes my core throb. "That's good," he says. "Since you picked my tux and all."

"I wanted us to match," I say with a shrug. When Gabi let me decide the color of the bridesmaids' dresses, I chose a dusty pink, which complimented her dress perfectly. And of course, I had to make the men match, so I had them wear a matching dusty pink pocket square.

Lucas hums, sliding a hand to clutch my face. "You did your job perfectly," he says. "We look like a match made in heaven." He leans down and brushes his lips against mine, our kiss soft and sweet and full of love.

I get lost in him, completely disregarding how long we stay here making out, or the fact that his hand is completely messing up my hair. "Lucas." I pull back with a hum, my vision a little hazy when I open my eyes to look up at him. "My hair," I murmur, reaching up to smooth it down, hoping it's not too messed up.

He chuckles, wiping a thumb over my lips, and that's when I remember my makeup is no doubt messed up too. "You're so fucking beautiful, *princesa*. I can't help it."

I shake my head at the same time as my lips curl into a smile. "You can mess it up later, I promise." I turn around to face the mirror, my eyes widening when I see the smudged lipstick, and my hair out of place. "We can't get off track," I tell him, fixing up my makeup. "Besides, we need to leave in …" I glance over at my phone, my eyes widening when I see the time. "Now."

"Right now?" he repeats, arching a brow. "Are you sure we don't have any time left?"

I let out a sigh, hating how well he knows me. "Fine, we need to leave in thirty-minutes. But I want to be there early," I say, picking up my perfume before spritzing some on my skin.

Lucas immediately buries his face in my neck, letting out a groan, and I chuckle as the vibrations of his voice ripple through my skin. "Lucas," I say, a little breathless as he starts to kiss all over my neck.

"Just two more minutes, baby," he murmurs, leaving soft kisses on my skin as his hands curl around my waist. "Let me just hold you for a bit."

My shoulders drop and I let my eyes fall closed as Lucas kisses me. But it doesn't last long before my phone goes off with a ring, and my eyes snap open.

"I swear if that's Gabi again," Lucas grunts.

I let out a chuckle, reaching for my phone. "She probably has a makeup emergency or—" I freeze, the words stuck in my mouth as I glance at the screen.

"What?" Lucas asks, stepping around me, with furrowed brows. "What is it?"

I slowly lift my head, the phone ringing between us, and swallow hard. "It's not Gabi."

His frown deepens. "Who is it?"

My heart is lodged in my chest as I hold up the phone to him, and see his eyes widen when he reads.

Lakeside Adoption Center

"Fuck."

My heart knocks loudly against my chest. "What do I do?" I ask, desperately as the phone continues to ring.

"Relax, *princesa*," Lucas says in a calm voice that makes my shoulders ease as he holds my face in his hands, and leans down for a soft kiss. "Everything is going to be okay. Just answer the phone, and *breathe*."

I stare at the phone ringing in my hand, and shake my head, feeling my whole body tense up. "I can't."

"Do you want me to answer it?" he asks.

I immediately nod, and Lucas takes the phone from my hand, and answers the call, bringing the phone to his ear. "Hello, this is Lucas Silva."

I watch as he listens intently to the other side, nodding a couple times, letting out a few 'mhmm' and then a, "Thank you so much."

When he hangs up the phone, he places it on the vanity, and grips the side, letting out a heavy breath.

"So?" I ask, feeling my heart lodged in my throat as he lifts his head and looks at me, the muscle in his jaw ticking. No. *No*. This can't be it.

Lucas steps away from the vanity, reaching for my hand, and brings it to his lips, kissing my knuckles. "Do you want to know now, or wait until after the wedding?" he asks.

There's no point in delaying the inevitable. I don't want to spend the whole wedding wondering, and hoping, and having my mind somewhere else. Tears build in my eyes as I shake my head. "Just tell me now," I tell him. "I can handle it," I lie, letting out a shaky breath. "I already knew this would happen."

This is exactly why I didn't want to put it out into the world. If I never let myself speak about what I wanted, I could pretend I didn't care that ultimately it would get taken away from me. But I *do* care. I care so much. I really wanted this. And it breaks my heart that my dream of having a family is crushed between my fingers.

"So did I," Lucas says, leaning in to kiss me which makes me break out into a sob. "I always knew we'd have a baby."

I pause, my head lifting to see Lucas with a smile on his face. "Wait." I blink away the tears, seeing his smile widen by the second. "What?" I ask, wondering if he really just said what I think he said.

"We got chosen, baby," he says with a huge smile as he leans down to kiss me.

"We… we did?"

He nods, rubbing his thumb over my cheeks. "Of course we did. I knew we would be. Samantha called, and said there is a baby that needs a home, and will be in touch soon to finalize the paperwork."

More tears fall down my face, and to hell with my makeup. I shake my head, unable to believe it. "We're going to have a baby?"

Lucas nods, his own eyes tearing up as he clutches my face in both of his hands, wiping away the tears. "We're going to have a baby," he confirms. "You're going to be a mom."

"And you're going to be a dad," I say, shakily as tears blind my vision. He nods, letting out a laugh before he leans down and kisses me. "I can't believe it," I murmur, still in complete disbelief.

"Believe it, *princesa*," he says, wiping away my tears. "There will still be a lot we need to do, but we're on our way, baby. We're going to have a family." He tucks a strand of hair behind my ear, his eyes locked on mine.

"This means we can start telling people, right?"

He nods. "We can tell our friends whenever we're ready." He lets out a chuckle. "I already know Adrianna is going to buy the baby a thousand different outfits."

A laugh bubbles out of me, knowing that's definitely true. When we told our family, they were all very supportive, but especially Adrianna. It's been amazing seeing Lucas's sister grow into the beautiful young woman she is today. And taking after Leila, she decided to start a fashion page, showing girls with all different body types that they can dress however they want.

And while I love her, she goes a little overboard. When we told her we were thinking of adopting, she went ahead and bought ten different outfits. It was a little hard seeing the clothes around the house since we didn't have a baby. But now, I can't wait to tell my child that their auntie Adri bought them their first clothes.

"You're an amazing actress, we're so close to having your dream house built, and now we're having a baby." His eyes are full of joy as his lips curve into a smile. "You're getting everything you ever wanted."

A long time ago, all I wanted was my career. I wanted to become an actress. I wanted to do what I loved, and I got it. And now…

"All I've ever wanted was you," I tell him, wrapping my arms around his neck. "Thank you for being the best part of my life."

His eyes tear up and he leans down to kiss me. "Thank you for being my life," he says. "I love you so much *princesa*, and I can't wait to build a family with you. I can't wait to see you be the best damn mother ever."

Chapter 17

"You've got everything you need in the diaper bag, right?"
The guys all smirk at Aiden freaking out over leaving Talia
with Leila's mom for the first time. "And the milk. It needs to
be at—I know you've taken care of babies before, I just
wanted to remind you." A sigh leaves him and he closes his
eyes. "Okay. Fine. I'm sorry. Tell my daughters I love them."
He hangs up the call and he wipes a hand down his face,
clearly exhausted.

"Breathe, man," Grayson says, tapping him on his back.
"She'll be okay."

He twists his head to look at him. "It's only been two days
since she was born," he says, with a slight shake of his head.
"It's really fucking hard being away from her."

"Gabi made it clear you guys could stay home with the
baby, she understands it's a big deal," Chris says,
understanding flashing in his eyes.

Gabi talks a big talk about being cutthroat but when it
comes to her friends, she'd do anything. She was even
considering changing her wedding day altogether, which gave
Madi a mini heart attack, but Leila and Aiden refused to be
the reason she delayed her wedding.

"You know we weren't going to miss your big day," Aiden
replies with a smile. "Besides, Leila's mom is right. She's
taken care of babies before. Talia will be fine."

Grayson lifts his chin toward Chris. "How are you feeling? Nervous at all?" he asks.

Chris's lips curve into a smile as he shakes his head. "Not really," he replies with a shrug. "I've been ready to marry her for as long as I can remember."

Grayson nods, a smile creeping up on his face. "I know how you feel," he says, no doubt thinking of Rosie.

"I can't fucking wait to call her 'my wife'," Chris replies, tugging on the lapels of his tux in the mirror before he runs a hand through his hair, smiling at his reflection. "I remember a time when I'd give up my life for this to happen, and now it finally is."

Aiden lets out a chuckle. "Trust me, I know what you mean. I abuse that phrase very chance I get. In interviews, I never fail to mention *my wife*, whenever Leila's acting up, I make sure to remind her she's *my wife*." He shakes his head, a stupid grin on his face. "I really fucking love saying it."

James lets out a scoff. "I swear that's the only reason you got married so quickly."

Aiden chuckles. "You might be onto something," he says, before he shakes his head. "Mostly I just wanted to see my ring on her finger, to know she's mine and I'm hers, to be owned by her, and I wanted it to be legally binding so she could never leave me," he adds.

"She will never leave you," Grayson reassures him. "You've been hers since the day you guys met."

Aiden's face twists into a wince. "Not quite," he says. "I had to work for it, pretty hard." He looks into space, probably remembering when they first got together. "Worth it, though."

My phone vibrates in my pocket, and I pull it out, seeing my wife's name on the screen.

Aiden's right. I love saying *my wife*.

Princesa:

> Have you told them yet?

Lucas:

> Not yet. I'll tell them now.

Princesa:

> Good luck. I love you.

Lucas:

> I love you.

I pocket my phone, and my jaw tightens before I lift off the couch, and let out a breath, everyone's eyes on me when I do. "I have something I need to tell you guys."

I catch James's brows shooting up, knowing about mine and Madi's decision to adopt, and probably wondering if that's what I need to tell them.

I clear my throat, pulling on my shirt collar, suddenly feeling very fucking hot in this tux. "As some as you might now, Madi and I have been trying to have a baby for quite a while," I say, seeing Grayson's apologetic look. "We've uh... been to a lot of doctors, and done a lot of tests and..." I shake my head. "It hasn't happened yet."

Aiden's brows shoot up with understanding. "You guys can't have kids?" he guesses.

"I mean, it hasn't been confirmed," I tell him. "The tests come back fine, and the doctors tell us to keep trying, but it's been three years," I admit. "And if I'm honest, we kind of ditched the condoms and birth control before then, and yet…" I shrug.

"Fuck," Aiden replies, swallowing hard, his face turning pale. "I'm so sorry. All those times I asked… Is Madi okay?"

"Yeah," I confirm with a nod. "She was a little upset about all the questions, and seeing a new baby, but she's okay." Fuck. This is it. "We actually have some news."

"Wait. What?" James asks, confused since I haven't told him this yet.

"Madi and I decided on adoption a while back," I tell the guys. "We wanted to give a child a loving home, and this morning," I start, unable to keep the smile off my face. "We received a call letting us know there's a baby waiting for us."

"Holy shit," James says, his eyes widening. "You're serious?"

"Yep," I affirm with a laugh as the guys all smile.

"You're going to be a dad," Aiden says with a grin. "Join the fucking club."

I let out a laugh, nodding. "If everything goes well, then yes. It's a long process, and things could still fall apart and—"

"Hey," Grayson cuts in, tapping on my shoulder. "Don't say that. Everything is going to go perfectly. You guys were meant to be parents."

A weight lifts off my shoulder and I smile at the guys. "Thanks, you guys."

"Holy fuck. I can't believe there's going to be another baby around here," James says, sounding a little shocked, and a little scared, too.

"You're going to be an uncle," I say, pulling him in for a hug.

"I'm too young for that," he cries out.

"We need a drink to celebrate," Chris says, heading out into the hallway.

I pull away from the guys to reach into my pocket, typing out a text with a smile on my face.

Lucas:

I told them.

Princesa:

I figured. We heard loud noises.

Lucas:

Have you told the girls yet?

Princesa:

Not yet. I'm nervous.

Lucas:

There's no reason to be. They're going to be supportive, baby. Good luck. I love you.

Princesa:

I love you too.

I pocket my phone when Chris walks back into the room with champagne glasses, and one filled with what looks like orange juice for Aiden.

"Congrats man," he says, handing me the glass.

"To Lucas and Madi," Grayson says, raising his glass in a toast.

I let out a laugh as the guys toast, and cheer, and I smile, looking around at the amazing friends I've managed to gain.

I can't wait to introduce my baby to their amazing uncles.

And I can't wait to build a family with my wife.

Chapter 18

MADELINE

"What the hell was that?" Gabi asks, lifting her head from the mirror to look at the door where the loud noise of the guys' cheering came from. "Are they watching a game or something?" A groan leaves her lips. "*Men*. I mean come on, it's my wedding. They couldn't have waited until later?" She shakes her head, dropping her eyes to the mirror to fix her hair.

A smile creeps on my face, knowing the noise wasn't because they were watching a game, but because Lucas told them we're going to be parents.

"What the hell were you doing this morning?" Leila asks, trying to fix my smudged makeup.

"I bet they were fucking," Gabi adds with a smirk. "You guys are kinky, aren't you?" she asks, tilting her head at me, which I reply with a scowl.

"Shouldn't you know the answer to that?" Rosie asks, letting out a laugh. "You walked in on them once, right?"

Gabi groans, meeting my eyes. "Twice."

Leila pauses doing my makeup, turning to face Gabi. "Twice?"

Gabi nods, and blinks at me. "They were fooling around in the bathroom last night."

"Damn," Leila says, lifting her brows. "That's hot. I didn't know you guys were like that."

My cheeks heat up and I roll my eyes. "Oh, please. You guys are on your second baby. Like you can talk." Leila lets out a soft chuckle, and returns to doing my makeup. "Besides, Gabi didn't see anything. She walked in when we were already done," I add with a smirk.

"Believe me, I did. It's burned into my mind. I've talked to my therapist about it. It's scarred me for life," she says, a disgusted expression taking over her features. "When you guys were dating in college, I walked into the living room and saw skin and heard moans, and I swear I blacked out," she says, groaning. "It was traumatizing."

Leila snickers. "I kind of thought that would be something you enjoyed."

"Seeing my best friend who's practically another sister getting fucked wasn't high on my bucket list," she adds.

I arch a brow. "I'm practically your sister?"

She gives me a dry look. "That's all you heard?"

I nod, letting out a chuckle. "Gabi's being so sweet today," I joke, seeing her lips lift into a smile.

"I'm always sweet," she says, leaning back into her chair.

Leila hums. "This weekend you've been kind of bossy," she says.

Gabi's brows furrow. "I have?"

"She's a bride," I say. "It's normal."

Gabi lets out a scoff. "Exactly. It's normal," she repeats. "Besides, you were worse than I was at my wedding."

"How was I worse?" Leila asks with a laugh.

Gabi tilts her head. "Your wedding planner quit three weeks before, and Madi had to take over," she says.

Leila rolls her eyes. "She was weak," she says, turning back around to apply some powder under my eyes. "If you're going to work with brides, then you need to have a backbone."

Gabi snickers, shaking her head, and Leila pulls back, reaching for her phone, which is vibrating beside her. When she opens her phone, I notice the sad look on her face.

"Talia?" I guess, imagining it's hard for her to leave her baby so soon.

Leila nods, letting out a sigh. "My mom's texting me updates and pictures and… I miss her so much."

"I can imagine," I say, reassuringly.

"But I know she'll be fine," Leila says, letting out a breath as she places her phone beside her. "And I'm really excited for Nova to have some time with her baby sister."

"How did she react when she met her?" Rosie asks, her eyes lighting up. I wonder when her and Grayson will have kids. I hope it's much easier for them than it has been for Lucas and me.

"She cried," Leila adds, tears building up in her eyes. "She rarely ever cries, and she bawled her eyes out when she saw her sister, saying she loved her. Fuck."

"Don't cry," I say, feeling my own tears start to build. "We can't all show up with ruined makeup. *Breathe*," I order her, fanning her face, until the tears start to go back into her body.

"As much as I love the talk of babies, it's kind of making me nauseous. Can we please move on?" Gabi asks.

I glance over at her, and a smile creeps up on my face. This is the perfect time to tell them. "Actually…" I start, feeling my heart knock against my chest.

"Oh god. You're pregnant, aren't you?" Gabi asks.

The knocking increases, and I shake my head. "No, I'm not."

"Phew," she says, closing her eyes.

"I actually can't get pregnant."

Gabi freezes, her eyes widening when she looks back at me. "Wait. What?"

"Fuck," Leila says. "Please say you're kidding."

I shake my head. "There's nothing inherently wrong according to the doctors, but we've been trying for a while, and… I really don't know if it will ever happen for us. But…"

"But?" Leila asks, lifting her brows.

I take a deep breath in, squaring my shoulders. "Lucas and I decided to adopt a while back."

Gabi's eyes widen. "You did?"

I nod in confirmation. "I'm really sorry I didn't tell you girls before, but I didn't want to say anything before anything was concrete," I admit. "I didn't want the pressure, or questions, or for you guys to look at me like I was a failure," I say, my voice cracking on the last word.

Gabi lifts off her chair, coming to sit beside me, and places her hand on my shoulder. "You could never be a failure," she says.

"We completely understand why you didn't want to tell anyone," Rosie adds, her blue eyes glassy.

"Wait," Leila says, her brows knitting together. "You just said you didn't want to tell us before anything was concrete. So, if you're telling us now, does that mean…"

I nod, my smile widening on my face. "We're getting a baby."

"Oh my god," Gabi gasps, and I notice her eyes brimming with tears. "Wait. Really?"

I nod, letting out a laugh. "We got the call this morning," I tell them. "And the loud noise you heard from the guys just now wasn't from a game they're watching, but from Lucas telling them about the adoption."

"What?" Gabi says, furrowing her brows. "I can't believe they found out before me." Leila clears her throat, and Gabi rolls her eyes. "Us," she corrects.

"I was really nervous," I admit to them. "I needed Lucas to tell them first. But I'm so happy I finally told you guys."

"You're going to be a mom," Leila says, with a smile on her face.

The word lights up my chest, and I let myself accept it, nodding. "I am."

"We can have playdates," she replies, nudging me on the arm.

"That sounds boring," Gabi adds.

"Well since you don't have a child yet, you won't be invited to the playdates," Leila says with an amused look.

Gabi's mouth drops. "But I make really good imaginary tea."

We all laugh at Gabi's antics, and she smiles at me. "I'm really happy for you, Madi. You're going to be an amazing mother."

"Thank you."

I reach for my phone and start typing out a text to Lucas, with a smile on my face I can't—and don't want to—get rid of.

Madeline:

We did it. We've told our friends.

Lucas:

Up next is our parents, but that will be easy.

Madeline:

It's official.

Lucas:

We're going to be parents.

I break out into a grin at his text, but my attention is pulled away when I hear Gabi clearing her throat, and I look up to see her standing in the middle of the room, her hands fiddling with the tie of her dressing gown.

"I need to tell you guys something."

The Wedding

Chapter 19

GABRIELLA

"You look so beautiful."

I shift my gaze to the mirror, seeing the girls standing behind me, feeling tears threaten to spill. The look on their faces makes me turn around to face them, noticing the glassiness in their eyes as my vision starts to blur.

"No," Leila snaps, sniffing as she widens her eyes. "Don't you dare cry. Your makeup looks way too good to ruin it with tears."

I let out a laugh, attempting to make the tears go back inside. "I better not," I say, shaking my head. "I paid way too much for it."

She lets out a laugh, and Rosie hands me a napkin, which I reach for, wiping my eyes carefully.

"You're marrying your best friend," Madi says with a soft smile. "You shouldn't be crying."

"I know," I admit, though the thought makes my nose tingle with the tell-tale sign of tears. It doesn't make sense that I'd be crying over something I'm so excited about. "I can't believe the day is finally here," I admit with a quiet laugh. Ten years ago, I was madly in love with my best friend, and I never thought I would be standing here on my wedding day, about to marry him.

"You two were made for each other," Leila says with a subtle shake of her head, her eyes welling with tears. "I really do believe there are no two people more suited for each other than you and Chris."

Fuck. "Don't make me cry," I plead, my voice cracking as I feel the wetness build in my eyes.

She lets out a laugh, wiping under her eyes. "Sorry. I'm emotional. You know, the hormones and everything," she says, waving a hand.

Right. Of course.

"Okay, we've got to get going," Madi says, checking her phone. "It's about to start."

Rosie and Leila flash me a smile before heading out of the room, and as Madi is about to walk out, I grip onto her arm, and she turns around, confusion etched onto her features. "What's wrong?"

"Nothing," I say, shaking my head. "I just wanted to thank you for helping me out with everything." Her eyes soften and I let out a breath. "The wedding is so beautiful, Madi."

She rolls her eyes playfully, a smile spreading across her face. "This was all your wedding planner's doing," she says, which makes me let out a scoff.

"Please," I say, shaking my head. "We both know she did as much as *I* did," I say, arching a brow, which Madi laughs at. Truth is, Madi did more for this wedding, than my actual wedding planner did, and she's made my special day absolutely perfect.

"You deserve it," she says, placing her hand on mine.

I nod, swallowing hard. "Can I ask you for one last thing?"

She furrows her brows slightly, clearly worried. "Of course," she says. "Anything."

148

"I want to see Chris."

Her brows shoot up. "Right now?"

I nod, keeping my eyes on hers.

"Are you okay?" she asks, her eyes scanning my body. "Is it—"

"No," I say with a shake of my head. "I just really need to see him right now."

I notice her features tightening, but then she nods. "Okay. I'll see what I can do."

I watch as she walks out, closing the door behind her until I'm left alone. I breathe out a hard sigh, glancing at the mirror again.

But when a knock hits the door, I snap my head toward it. "Gabi?"

"Chris," I murmur, my shoulders falling as I hear his voice through the wooden door.

"I really want to come in, but I don't want to see your dress," he says which makes me smile.

I'm not really one for superstitions. Besides, we got a matching tattoo early on in our relationship, which is considered a bad omen, and we're still going strong. But I can tell he really cares about this.

"You can turn around," I tell him, my lips curling into a smile.

"Okay," I hear him say, watching as the door opens and he walks inside, backward. My smile widens when I glance at the back of his head as he breathes out, gripping his hair. "Are you okay?" he asks. "Please don't tell me you're having second thoughts."

"No," I affirm, walking toward him. "Never."

"Then why…" His words trail off when I reach for his hand, and he intertwines out fingers together, letting out a relieved sigh.

"I was just … feeling a little nervous," I tell him, and Chris squeezes my hand in his. "I just needed you."

"I need you too, pretty girl," Chris breathes out. "So fucking much." He lifts my hand to his lips, and presses a kiss against my knuckles. "Do you still want this? Do you still want to marry me?" he asks, his voice low, uncertain, like he's worried I'll say no. My heart aches for the love I have for this man, and the fact that he'd give me anything I wanted, even if I did want to call this whole thing off.

I wrap my arms around him, placing my forehead against his back. "More than anything."

I feel his shoulders slump with relief before he kisses my hand again. "Me too, baby. I can't wait to see you walk down that aisle."

I chuckle, lifting my head to look up at the back of his head. "Are you going to cry?" I ask him.

His shoulders shake with a laugh. "Probably."

A groan escapes me. "You know that if you cry, then I'll cry, and then I'll ruin my makeup."

He chuckles again. "You'll still be the most beautiful girl in the world."

My lips curve into a smile as I sigh. "I'll look like a racoon, Chris. I don't think you'd want to marry a racoon."

"You'd be a beautiful racoon," he says, which makes me roll my eyes. "And you already know I'd marry you no matter what you look like Gabi." He groans, shaking his head. "Fuck, I just want to kiss you right now."

I squeeze my eyes closed. "Me too." I don't want to wait until we get out there. I want to kiss him right now. I want to feel him. I just want *him*. "Wait," I say, snapping my eyes open and untangling myself from him. "I have an idea."

I head toward the vanity area, and grab my dressing gown tie, before I walk back toward Chris. Being a whole seven inches shorter than him, isn't going to make this easy, but I lift onto my tip-toes to reach the tie around his eyes, and tie it at the back of his head.

"There," I say, once I've tied off the makeshift blindfold. "You can turn around now."

He slowly turns around, reaching for me. As soon as his hands find my waist, he melts, gripping my body in his hands. "*Fuck*, baby."

I lift my arms, wrapping them around his neck. "Just kiss me already," I tease.

He lets out a laugh before leaning down and finding my lips, kissing me in a way I can feel down to my toes, my skin shivering with each lingering moment of his lips on mine. My hands find their way into his hair, gripping the strands as I move his head, deepening the kiss. It still feels like our first. Every single kiss we share feels like my heart is going to erupt the moment his lips land on mine.

But when a knock hits the door, we pull apart, heavy breaths leaving our lips as I stare down at him, his eyes covered with a white fluffy dressing gown tie.

"Gabi," Madi says, on the other side of the door. "We need to go."

Chris lets out a hard breath, his hand slowly making its way up my body until he cups my face, leaning down for another kiss. "I'll see you out there," he says. "Okay?"

My lips turn into a smirk as I let out a laugh. "If I don't run first."

He grips my waist, a low rough noise leaving his throat. "Don't even play about that," he pleads, shaking his head. "My heart's beating so fucking fast."

"I'll never leave you," I promise, holding his face in my hands before I lean down and kiss him one more time. "You're everything I've ever wanted."

"Fuck," he breathes out, dropping his head. "Please… just get out there so you can marry me already."

I let out a laugh against his lips. "I love you."

"I love you, pretty girl," he murmurs. "I can't fucking wait to call you my wife."

I reluctantly let my hands fall from him, and watch as he turns around, rips the blindfold off, and leaves the room, Jane, my sister walking in a second later.

"Are you ready to go?" she asks, nervously.

I let out a breath, squaring my shoulders. "Yes."

She tilts her head, examining me. "Are you sure?"

My brows furrow in amusement. "Do you not want me to be or…"

"I was just making sure," she says with a shrug. "I was really nervous on my wedding day," she admits, smiling at the reminder.

"Really?" My brows dip. I guess I was a little concerned with everything happening with Chris, I didn't really notice my sister being nervous. I don't think I've ever seen her be nervous. Controlling, demanding, bossy, yes. But nervous? She wasn't even nervous when our father kicked her out after she came out. She kept sane, and calm, and told me it was all going to be okay as I was bawling my eyes out.

"Of course I was," she admits. "But I'm your big sister. I'm never going to show you my weaknesses," she says, assertively.

I shake my head. "You were never weak," I tell her. "I always looked up to you."

She smiles, which turns into a knowing smirk. "I called it, by the way. I knew some day you two would end up together."

I breathe out a laugh. That's my sister. Always has to be right about everything. "Yeah, I know," I say, remembering all the times she'd say something about us being together. I used to shut her down back when I hadn't realized my feelings for him, but my sister knew before I did.

"I feel like I'm owed some kind of compensation for it," she says, arching a brow.

A laugh bubbles out of me. "How about you just watch me walk down the aisle to marry my best friend and we'll call it even?"

She sighs. "I guess." We share a smile, and she reaches out to fix my veil, making sure it's perfectly placed. "You look really beautiful, Gabi. Mom would have been so proud of the woman you've become."

My lips wobbles at the reminder of my mom, and this time, a tear does fall down my cheek. I remember her telling us about her wedding, and how she couldn't wait to see us, but she's not here. She won't see me getting married. She won't see me grow up. She'll never meet my children.

"No crying," my sister says, her own eyes full of tears as she wipes my cheek. "We need to go."

I sniff back the tears, and wrap my arm around my sister as we push through the doors.

Chapter 20

CHRISTOPHER

I'm going to throw up.

It's stupid when I think about it. There's no logical reason to be nervous. I'm about to marry my best friend. I've wanted this to happen since I was fifteen and gave her my hoodie for the first time. Gabi wearing something of mine on her made me want to give her *everything* that's mine. My clothes, my heart, my last name.

And now it's about to happen.

And yet my hands are shaking, and my brows are sweating. I didn't even know brows could sweat.

Fuck.

I turn my head when I feel a hand on my shoulder and meet Grayson's eyes. "Calm down, man. I can see you shake," he says with a hint of a smirk.

I nod, turning my head back to the entrance and try to calm down. My eyes meet my mom's as she smiles warmly at me, her husband sits beside her. Out family, and friends are all gathered here, for us, for me. And they're all looking right at me.

Christ. I run a hand through my hair as my tongue darts out, running along my lips, still tasting her sweet strawberry lip gloss. I almost want to reach my hand up and trace where her lips last were. That's my last kiss with my girlfriend. The next time I kiss her, she's going to be my wife.

The smile on my face slips, and panic settles over my body when I hear the music start as everyone stands from the white chairs with round gold borders Gabi and I picked out months ago.

Fuck. It's happening.

I shake my hands, glad that everyone is looking toward the door instead of at me. I'm not really a big people person, and standing up here, while everyone's eyes are on me makes me fucking twitch.

I just want my girl here.

I'm always okay when she's with me.

I shake my hands, blowing out a hard breath as I look toward the entrance of the venue, anticipating seeing her for the first time. Being in a blindfold nearly killed me when I finally turned around and felt her in that dress. All I wanted to do was see it, but damn if I was going to take any chances of bad luck for us.

I want all the luck and chances in the world when it comes to her. I never, in a million years, would have thought I'd be standing here with my best friend, the love of my life, about to marry her, ten years ago. And every day I pinch myself that it's real. That she's with me. That we're finally together.

So, hell no. I'm not taking any chances.

Rosie steps out, walking down the pathway, wearing a long muted pink dress, in a soft silk material, holding a bouquet of pink flowers. I turn my head, seeing Grayson watching her in awe. His smile is so wide, so bright, it catches me off guard. I don't think I've ever seen him smile like that in the years that I've known him. I have no doubt that he's thinking about what his own wedding will be like. What seeing Rosie in her wedding dress will feel like.

Rosie walks toward the left side, opposite us, as Leila walks out in a matching dress and bouquet, her eyes locked onto Aiden's. I don't even have to look to know his eyes are on her, too. They're always on her. I watch as her face lights up with a smile before she stands behind Rosie.

Madeline is next to walk out in the same dress and bouquet, and I've got to give her props for this whole thing. She's the reason this wedding is as beautiful as it is. I promised Gabi I'd always give her exactly what she wanted, and that included her dream wedding. I don't even know how many texts Madi received from Gabi over the last year about this wedding, but I've got to thank her for putting up with all of it, because it turned out so fucking great. It's perfect.

Madeline takes her place behind Leila, and my body tenses up. My bones freeze, my blood stops pumping and the heart beating in my chest comes to a halt.

And then I see her.

Holy fuck.

I feel the blood slowly pumping back into my veins as my heart bangs against my chest, beating back to life when she rounds the corner, and lifts her head.

Her blue eyes are immediately lock onto mine, and... fuck.

I told her I wouldn't cry, but there's nothing I can do to stop the tears falling down my face as I watch my best friend walking down the aisle toward me, taking step by step on top of the pink petals scattered on the ground.

I can see her sister guiding her from the corner of my eye, but I can't seem to look at anyone but Gabi. It's been like that since I was twelve, unable to understand why my heart would beat extra fast whenever she was around.

It's hard to look at anywhere but those gorgeous glassy blue eyes, but fuck. That dress. I can't help but look at the dress on her body. It's been such a mystery to me. Gabi kept teasing me, telling me I'd go crazy when I saw it, and holy shit, she was right.

I reach up, wiping a hand over my mouth as I watch her gorgeous white dress wrapped tightly around her body, and flow outward beautifully, covered in lace flower details. The neckline is teasing and fucking mouthwatering as her tits poke out of the strapless dress, curving slightly in the middle. Her hair is curled around her face, and a simple white veil flows behind her back.

Jesus.

Rosie fucking killed it at the design of the dress.

Gabi has always been beautiful. But today, she looks regal, angelic.

I can't fucking wait to rip that dress off—or gently take it off—her later tonight.

Fuck, how did I get so lucky?

I wipe my eyes as she reaches me, and I hold out my hand, guiding her to stand in front of me.

Her eyes are glassy as they meet mine. "You made me cry," she whispers, tears streaming down her cheeks.

I shake my head, apologetically. "I couldn't help it," I reply, swallowing down the hard rock lodged in my throat.

"You look so beautiful, pretty girl," I say, gently wiping her under eyes before I lean in and press my lips to her forehead.

I'm aware everyone here is watching us, but right now, it's just me and her, and I really needed to kiss my girl.

"Ladies and gentlemen, friends, and family," the officiant starts, and I reach for Gabi's hands, holding them in mine. "We are gathered here today to celebrate the union of Gabriella Miller and Christopher Hudson..."

The officiant trails off as I look into Gabi's eyes, unable to keep the smile off my face. Her eyes are magical, I swear. I look into them, and everything bad in my life is completely erased. Even back when I was a scared teenager, running away from my dad, as soon as she looked at me, he completely ceased to exist. I wasn't getting beaten, I wasn't scared, and I wasn't running away. I was just me. And she... was everything.

And even now, when my eyes are on hers, no one but us exists. The whole place is empty. There's no one else here, not even the officiant. It's just me and her.

Just us.

I squeeze her hand in mine, trying my hardest to tell her with my eyes that she is the best thing that ever happened to a kid like me. I wonder what would have happened if we never met that day in the skate park. If we'd never met at all. I genuinely think a part of me wouldn't exist. Not without her.

I would go back to that very first time and scrape my knee every chance I could if it meant we got to be here together in the end.

Gabi is my beginning and my end. She's my heaven and my earth. She's the stars in the sky and the sun when it shines. She's everything. My whole life.

"Gabriella Miller," the officiant says, snapping me out of our moment. "Do you take Christopher Hudson to be your lawfully wedded husband, to have and to hold, from this day forward, for better or for worse, for richer or for poorer, in sickness and in health, to love and to cherish, until death do you part?"

She holds my eyes, her gorgeous glossy pink lips curving when she says, "I do."

"And do you, Christopher Hudson, take Gabriella Miller to be your lawfully wedded wife, to have and to hold, from this day forward, for better or for worse, for richer or for poorer, in sickness and in health, to love and to cherish, until death do you part?"

I run my thumb over her engagement ring, before I scoot my hand up, tracing our matching tattoo on the inside of her wrist. "I do."

"It is my honor to pronounce you as husband and wife. You may now kiss the bride."

I slide a hand across her neck, cupping her face in my hand before I lean forward and kiss my wife for the very first time, in a way that's definitely indecent, considering we're standing in front of our family. But I couldn't give a fuck.

I've waited for this moment way too long to care about what anyone else thinks.

Gabi is my wife.

My hands tug at her waist until I wrap them around her and lift her into my arms, a soft yelp leaving her lips before she laughs into my mouth, wrapping her legs around my waist.

I kiss her like it's the first time. I kiss her like I'll never kiss her again. I kiss her with everything I have, and everything I am, and everything we're going to be.

When we pull apart, she throws her head back letting out a laugh that knocks me in the chest. It's still my favorite sound in the world. I want her to be this happy every second of the day, and I will do anything I can to make that possible. All I want is her happiness.

"I love you, pretty girl," I murmur, clutching her face in my hand as I press our foreheads together, wanting to be as close to her as physically possible.

"I love you," Gabi replies, pulling back to meet my eyes, a smirk twitching on her lips. "*Husband.*"

Fuck.

I pull her into me, kissing her hard, again, a need building up inside of me for her.

"Alright," Aiden says with a chuckle, patting me on my back, causing up to break apart. "You kids better calm down before you end up conceiving a baby right here."

Gabi rolls her eyes, her hands still wrapped around my neck, and her legs around my waist. "That would never happen."

His chest shakes with a laugh, and he shakes his head. "With you guys?" he says, tilting his head at us. "Anything is possible."

He walks away, sneaking up behind Leila to wrap his arms around her, and I turn back around to face my beautiful wife, best friend, and the love of my life, all in one amazing person.

"Did you hear that?" I say, arching a brow teasingly as I tuck a strand of hair behind her ear. "Anything is possible."

Chapter 21

GABRIELLA

The sunset washes over us, the orange pink hue painting a beautiful scene, as Chris spins me around, pulling me into him a second later.

A laugh bubbles out of me as I grip onto his shoulders. "Wow. The dance lessons we took really paid off," I tease, as his hands tighten on my waist.

He arches a brow. "You're acting like we haven't practiced dancing since we were kids," he says with a smirk. "Well, you more than me, but…"

"You mean when I forced you?" I ask, reminding him of the time I practically dragged him up from the floor when we were both high, and drunk, and tired as fuck, and I made him dance with me.

He tugs on my waist, pulling me flush against him, and locks his eyes with mine. "You could never force me to do anything, Gabi. You know I'd do anything you wanted, no matter what." I suck in a breath keeping my eyes on his chocolate ones I love so much. "No forcing needed."

His lips curve the tiniest bit, making my heart pound against my chest. How was I so stupid so for long? How in the hell did I not know that Chris was everything I have ever wanted, and needed for the first six years of our friendship? It's so clear to me now how perfect he is. How perfect we are together. How there's no one in the whole entire planet that could make me feel like he does.

I shake my head slightly, my heart fluttering like crazy. "Why are you so perfect?" I ask him.

He lets out a low chuckle while we continue to dance, stepping to the slow song we both picked out to be our first dance. "I'm definitely not," he says with a smirk.

I shake my head again, sliding my hand from his shoulder to the back of his neck, letting my fingers get tangled in his curly hair. "You're perfect for me," I tell him because everything in me screams for him. Every breath I take, every step I take, every damn morning I wake up the only thing that matters to me is this man right in front of me.

Chris comes to a halt, his hand falling from mine to clutch my face, his eyes scanning mine for what feels like eternity before he leans down and presses his lips to mine, deep and slow and full of passion. I'm aware everyone is watching us, since we're the only people on the dancefloor, but I don't care. This is my day. Our day. And I'm going to kiss my husband however many times I please.

When Chris pulls back, his lips curve into a smile, and he traces my cheek with the pad of his thumb, holding my face in the palm of his hand. "That's all I've ever wanted to be," he says making my heart thud against my chest.

"Alright," the DJ says, breaking the moment between us. "I think it's time for everyone else to join the happy couple."

I turn my head, spotting a couple of people stepping away from their table to join me and Chris. I even see Chris' mom join the dancefloor with her husband, both of them smiling at each other as they dance together.

I look around the gorgeous venue we picked out months ago, all our friends and family surrounding us, sitting on the gold chairs I was dying to have, and eating the expensive as fuck salmon that looked way too fancy for me, and I can't help but smile as I lay my head on Chris's chest.

"Everything is so perfect," I murmur as we continue to slow dance, pressed against each other. "This is the best wedding I could ever ask for."

I feel his thumb gently lift my chin and I turn to look up at him as he smiles down at me with those kind eyes. "I'm glad you love it, pretty girl. I want to make you this happy forever."

My lips part. "Forever's a long time," I say.

He nods. "But not long enough with you."

God. This man knows all of the right words to make me melt into a puddle. I love him so much. "Do you want kids?" I blurt out before my brain can catch up.

Chris pauses, his brows slightly furrowing as he searches my eyes. "Where is this coming from?" he asks.

I shrug, feeling my stomach churn. "I don't know. It was just something I was wondering about."

He arches a brow, still watching me unconvinced. "Do you want kids?"

I pause, thinking about every possible answer I could give him. "Maybe."

"Maybe," he repeats, a slight smirk on his lips. "You don't sound too sure."

A sigh leaves my lips, and I turn to face him. "I don't want my answer to influence you. I want to know what you think," I tell him. "I already know you'd give me anything I wanted, but I need to know, Chris," I say, swallowing hard. "I need to know if you really want kids."

He watches me for a while, people dancing around us. It might have been a better idea to wait until we were at the hotel, or maybe even before we got married, but the thought is killing me, and I need to know his answer right now before I go insane.

He finally lets out a sigh, and closes his eyes briefly. "Of course I do, Gabi. Are you kidding? Seeing a little baby with both of our features would be fucking amazing," he says which makes me suck in a breath. "It wouldn't be easy, of course, but I work from home so I could take care of them while you were working. We'd go to the park on the weekends, and have ice cream, and I'd teach them to play video games." He takes a breath. "I'd show them what real love from a father was, because it's something I never had." His eyes shift to mine, holding eye contact. "And I would love to see you as a mom," he continues. "You'd be so fucking great. They'd have so much fun and love, and of course you'd burn their birthday cake."

"Hey," I interrupt with narrowed eyes. "You said I'm getting better at baking."

"I lied," he says with a teasing smirk as he caresses my cheek with his thumb. "I'd love to see you love our baby," he continues. "We'd have sleepovers, and watch Disney movies, and… yes, Gabi. I would love to have kids with you," he affirms. "But I'm not going to let my wants influence *your* decision. This isn't a dealbreaker for me. I just want you. I have always just wanted *you*. And I'm good with whatever comes with it, I'm locked for life, baby. I'm here to stay."

His answer catches me off guard, and I swallow, feeling my throat tighten. "You've really thought about it."

He lets out a low scoff, shaking his head. "I don't do much except think about you," he says, leaning down to press his lips softly against my forehead.

When I pull back, I glance up at him, getting lost in his eyes. Until I see Grayson… dancing. My eyebrows shoot up, and Chris turns around, following my gaze.

"Is Grayson dancing?" I ask, hearing Chris laugh as we both watch Grayson spin Rosie around, dancing with her with the biggest smile on his face.

Chris chuckles, watching them both. "I don't know why you're surprised. He'd do anything for his girl," he says, before glancing down at me. "I know the feeling."

Our eyes meet, and I lift my chin as he leans down ready to kiss me and—

"Aunt Gabi!"

I pull back, glancing at the little kid running toward me with her arms out wide. God, children are such cockblocks. She's lucky she's adorable.

"Hi cutie," I say with a laugh as she wraps her arms around my dress, secretly praying her hands aren't dirty because… this was an expensive dress.

"Wow," she says, her head tilted all the way back to look up at me, her big green eyes wide as hell. "You look like a princess."

"Thank you," I say, booping her on the nose. "I know."

Leila lets out a scoff, crossing her arms. "I'm her mother and she ran to you first," she says, shaking her head. "Un-freaking-believable."

I let out a laugh, smoothing my hands over Nova's silky smooth, mousy brown hair. "She likes me better," I tease. "You can't fault the girl. She has good taste."

"I feed her, and bathe her, and put her to sleep, but *suuuure*, you're her favorite," Leila says with an eye roll.

Aiden chuckles behind her, placing a kiss on the top of her head. "Don't be jealous, baby. She adores you."

"Not enough it seems like," Leila replies with a huff.

"Nova," Aiden calls, making her little head turn around to face them. "You love your mommy, don't you?"

Nova nods her head. "Yes. Mommy's sooo beautiful," she says, which makes my heart ache. God, kids are really fucking cute after all.

"See, gorgeous," Aiden says, wrapping his arms around her waist, leaning down to press a kiss to her cheek. "Our daughter loves you. She's just a little obsessed with Gabi right now," he says with a chuckle.

I feel a little hand tugging at my dress, and I look down seeing her big green eyes on me. "Is Uncle Chris your prince?" she asks, making Chris chuckle beside me.

"Yes," I say with a nod, sitting down and pulling her onto my lap. "He saved me from a big ugly dragon stepmother, and there was lava and an evil apple and stuff."

Chris arches his brow. "I think you're getting the stories mixed up," he says, amused.

I wave a hand. "It's all the same thing."

"Am I going to have a prince like Uncle Chris when I grow up?" Nova asks.

I want to tell her that my prince is one in a million. That there's no one like him in the entire world, but seeing as she's only four, and I don't want to blow her tiny head off I go another route. "If you want to," I tell her with a shrug. "Or you can have a princess instead."

"Really?" she asks, furrowing her little brows.

I let out a laugh. Might be too much for a kid to handle just yet. "Have you met your little sister yet?" I ask her.

She nods, a smile lighting up her face. "She looks like one of my dolls," she tells me. "Mommy said we can play together when she grows up." But then her smile slips a little. "She cries a lot."

I let out a scoff as Leila takes a seat beside me, watching me with a grin. "You're really good at this, you know?"

I glance down at little Nova with a smile. "I guess I am."

"No way. You're not backing down." Our attention is drawn as the guys join us, Grayson breaking out into a grin. "I'm too fucking excited to see this."

"Grayson," Leila snaps, her eyes narrowing before she gestures to Nova sat on my lap.

"Fu—I mean fudge. I'm sorry. I didn't notice," he says, apologetically.

"What are you excited to see?" I ask the guys as they join our table.

"You remember the bet about the baby?" Aiden asks, taking a seat beside his wife. "James double-downed and said he'd take five shots if he was wrong."

"That's not that bad," I say with a scoff. That used to be a calm night for me back in college.

Grayson arches his brow. "Five shots of tequila."

"Jesus," I cringe, shaking my head. "You're so dead."

He laughs nervously. "It was just a joke. I always knew it would be a girl."

Aiden laughs. "Sure you did, bud."

He drops his head, letting out a defeated groan. "Please don't make me do this," he pleads.

"You're not allowed to back out now. You're doing those shots."

James groans again, gripping onto his husband's suit. "Help me," he murmurs.

Carter laughs, tapping him on his back. "Here, let's go get cake."

"Ooh," he says, lifting his head. "Alright."

Chris lets out a laugh as he grabs a chair and sits down beside me, my head immediately dropping onto his shoulder.

"She's so quiet," he says, his eyes on Nova as she plays with my dress, murmuring to herself. "You think ours will be like that?"

Ours. My heart pounds as I turn my head, meeting his eyes. "No," I say with a smirk. "I think ours will be loud, and fun, and crazy."

Chris's smile widens as he slides a hand to cup my face. "Just like her mom," he says, leaning down to kiss me. "I can't wait."

"When can we leave?" I ask him when we pull back from our kiss.

He laughs. "Baby, it's our wedding."

"Which means we can leave early, right?" I say, hopeful, but the shake of his head makes my shoulders slump.

"Not quite," he says, his lips twitching. "We still have the toast and speeches, and I want to dance with you again." His smile slips a little. "What's up?" he asks. "Why do you want to leave already?"

I shrug, keeping my eyes on his. "I just want to be alone with you," I tell him.

He leans in, kissing me again, once, twice, short quick kisses that make my body shiver all the way down to my toes, wanting more. "There's no rush, pretty girl. We have the rest of our lives."

I groan. "You were right earlier. It's not enough when it comes to you."

His smile widens. "We'll have the afterlife too."

My brows knit together. "You think you're going to turn me good, Hudson? Forget it."

His shoulders shake with a laugh and she shakes his head. "If not, then I'll go down with you," he says. "As long as I'm with you, it will be heaven to me."

171

Chapter 22

CHRISTOPHER

I've been to quite a few weddings in my life. The first one was my mom's wedding to the man she always deserved. It was great, honestly. Quiet, intimate.

Leila and Aiden's was the complete opposite. It was huge, and expensive as fuck, and had way too many people. They had a blast, though, so that's all that really matters.

Carter and James's was more intimate, too, as was Lucas and Madi's.

I might be a little biased, but I've got to admit, my wedding was the best one I have ever attended. Hands down.

Not only did I make sure Gabi got everything she wanted—from the venue, and the food, down to her dream dress—we invited the people who mattered the most to us. Every person who attended our wedding was someone we both loved.

It was fucking amazing. Add in the fact that I got to marry my best friend, and we've got a winner.

And even now, not even five-minutes into the drive back to the hotel, my wife is already trying to defile me in this limo.

Best. Wedding. Ever.

"God, you're so hot," she mumbles into my mouth as she unbuttons my shirt, making me groan into her mouth.

"Baby," I murmur between kisses.

"Hmmm?"

"We're in public," I manage to say when she leans down and runs her tongue over the ripples of my stomach.

"We're in a car," she replies, continuing to unbutton my shirt.

"Which has a driver," I try to say, my head dizzy and my body aching for her, unable to think properly when she kisses me.

"He can't see us," she says, working my belt off. "Or hear us."

I groan. Highly fucking doubt that. How soundproof are these things anyway? What if he has a secret camera in here, or microphone, and is secretly recording this?

Gabi lifts her head, making my snap out of my thoughts. "Do you want your cock in my mouth or not?"

Christ.

My jaw clenches as I think over the million and one reasons why we shouldn't be doing this, but then I look at my beautiful wife, heat swimming in her eyes and I throw it all out the window.

"Fuck it," I say, gripping her waist before I pull her onto me, her thighs spreading open to straddle me. I curl a hand around her neck and pull her down, our lips meeting in a hot kiss as she continues to work my belt, pulling it off a second later.

Fuck, I want to feel her. My hands fumble around, attempting to lift her wedding dress that's drowning us as she grinds down onto my cock, making me moan into her mouth. *Fuck yes.* I grip her waist tighter, helping her grind down onto me as her arms wrap around my neck, kissing me deep as every brush of her pussy against my cock makes me light the fuck up.

I need closer, deeper, but I don't know where the dress starts, and where she ends. "Fuck, this is a lot of dress," I say, trying to move it out of the way.

"Don't rip it," she warns, grinding down on me. "It was very expensive, and might come in handy for my next wedding."

The teasing smile on her lips makes me narrow my eyes as I grip her waist, and flip us around, until her back is pressed against the leather seats, and I'm crowding her. "Don't even joke about that."

She laughs, running her hands over my hair. "I like seeing you jealous."

"You want to drive me crazy, huh?" I ask her, parting her legs with my thigh, slowly lifting her dress until I can see her lacy white panties that pull a groan deep from my throat.

"Yes," she gasps when I run my finger along the lacy material.

"Needy little thing," I murmur, pulling the material to the side, until I can see her pretty pink pussy slick with juices. Completely unable to resist her, I run my finger along her pussy, before slowly thrusting it inside her. "Fuck you're drenched," I husk out, dying to taste her, to feel her. There isn't enough room back here, and seeing as we're almost at the hotel, it'd be fucking torturous to start something I couldn't finish.

"Chris," she gasps, tilting her head back as I crook my finger inside her, my thumb slowly rubbing circles over her sweet clit.

"You're almost there, baby?" I ask her, slipping another finger inside her when I feel her walls tighten around my fingers.

"Yes," she says, squeezing her eyes as she grips onto my arm. "Please," she moans, moving her hips as my fingers reach exactly where she needs me to. Her body tightens up, her lips part and I can tell she's about to come, when the car comes to a halt.

Her eyes snap open when I pull out of her, and they widen as she glances around the stopped car. "*No*," she says, shaking her head. "No. I was *so* close."

I smirk, unable to resist a taste as I suck my fingers into my mouth. "That's too bad."

Her lips part as she lets out a deep breath, and narrows her eyes at me. "You dick."

I let out a chuckle, leaning close to her. "You want my dick, baby?" I ask, kissing her briefly.

She moans into my mouth, her fingers tangling in my hair, gripping tightly. "Chris, please," she begs, making me fucking shiver.

"You know that hearing you beg makes me weak to my knees," I tell her, buttoning up my shirt. "But the car's stopped. We're at the hotel."

"I don't care," she says, attempting to unbutton my shirt again. "I want you."

I let out a laugh, tugging her toward me, before I open the door and carry her out. "I'll make it up to you," I tell her, lowering her to the ground before I kiss her forehead and make her look a little less disheveled. "I promise."

She lets out a sigh, but behaves as we check into the hotel, and before we know it, we're pushing the door open to our hotel suite, my eyebrows lifting when I see a bunch of roses and chocolates spread out on the bed.

Gabi doesn't seem to care about any of the fancy shit, though, because as soon as the door closes behind us, she tugs on the collar of my shirt, her eyes pinned on mine. "You said you'd make it up to me," she reminds me, making me laugh at her eagerness.

I lift her into my arms, walk toward the bed, and drop her on the mattress, watching with a huge fucking smile as my dream woman scoots back, and throws all the shit on the bed off, clanking to the ground as she never once leaves my gaze.

When I start to lift her dress, my mouth waters at the sight, and I groan, gripping her thighs. "Fuck, Gabi. I can't wait to be inside you."

She lets out a heavy breath, shaking her head as she leans up on her elbows. "Not yet," she says, spreading her legs wider on the bed. "I want your mouth first."

Fuck. I can't believe this is my life.

"Fucking fine by me," I tell her, ripping off my tie before I start to unbutton my shirt, flinging it across the room a few seconds later. "I'm dying to taste my wife's pussy."

As soon as I've got my shirt off, I kick my pants off, until I'm buck naked, stroking my cock at the sight of my wife lying in bed, with her pretty little dress on. Gabi starts to attempt to shuffle out of her dress, but I stop her.

"Let me take it off," I tell her, my voice husky from pleasure. "I want to be the one to strip you down." I lean down, unzipping her dress—very fucking carefully considering how much this cost—and my throat tightens as the dress slips off, leaving her in a matching pair of white lacy lingerie.

I shake my head, a groan leaving my throat. "Fuck, Gabi." I don't waste any time before I grip her thighs apart and drop to my knees to ravage her, French kissing the drenched lacy material, hardly covering her sweet pussy.

"God," she moans, her hand tangling in my hair. "I need closer."

I pull back, and hook my fingers on the hem of her panties, sliding them down her legs, before placing her feet back on the bed, spreading out her legs until she's completely bare to me, glistening, drenched, and so fucking pretty I'm about to go mad.

I can't look at her and not want to devour that gorgeous pussy. And I do just that, shuffling on the ground, grabbing a handful of her ass in each of my hands to pull her closer to me until I kiss her pussy, soft at first, teasing, slow, fucking delicious.

"Make me come," she begs, starting to close her thighs around my head.

She does that whenever it's too much for her, when she's done with the teasing and just wants to come, but she's not getting what she wants tonight.

"I'm not rushing this, Gabi," I tell her, pulling back an inch to spread her thighs wide open again, falling to the bed. I lean down and press the softest kiss to her inner thighs, bringing out a soft moan from her lips. "This is our first night being married," I remind her. "I want to take every second slowly," I say, pressing soft kisses to her thighs after every word. I know I'm driving her crazy, and the feeling is fucking mutual as my cock presses against my pants.

She groans. "I hate going slow," she whines.

I hum against her skin, smelling how wet she is, dying for a taste of her. "Patience, baby," I murmur. "I want to make you come over," I say, flicking my tongue over her clit. "And over." Another lick. "And over." This time I wrap my lips around her clit and suck it into my mouth. "Until we both can't take it anymore," I say, rubbing my two middle fingers over her wetness before I thrust them inside her in one go, crooking them until she moans loudly. "And then," I continue, crooking my fingers inside of her as I continue to tease her clit with my tongue. "I'll slide deep inside of you, fucking you until you can't think, or breathe, or do anything but come all over my cock."

As soon as the words are out of my mouth, her thighs tighten around me again, and she throws her head back, letting out a loud moan, my fingers getting coated with her orgasm.

I almost grin at how easy that was, and how I'm dying to make it happen again.

"That's it, baby. You're going to give me one more."

"God, you're going to kill me," she says on a rough moan, thrusting her hips up as I continue to lick her clit.

178

"Not until you come on my tongue again," I tell her, holding her waist with one hand as I keep my fingers inside of her, and eat her pussy, kissing and sucking and licking until she's moaning again, her legs shaking as her second orgasm of the night crashes into her.

I keep licking her, sucking on her sweet clit as she shakes, overstimulated. She tastes so fucking good. It's hard to think of a reason to stop.

I pull away from her when she twitches one too many times, and stroke my aching hard cock at the sight of her. Eating her pussy makes me so fucking hard. Gabi's eyes zone in on my hand working over my cock, and they burn with need as she sits on her knees, scooting toward me.

I walk toward her, slowly stroking my cock, breathless grunts leaving my throat. "Open your mouth. Show me that pretty tongue."

She sticks her tongue out, those bright blue eyes locking with mine as I continue to stroke my cock, groaning at the sight of her. Gabi leans forward, capturing the tip of my cock in her mouth as she gives it a slow, hard suck, making my head lull back.

It isn't long until she takes over, wrapping her fist around my cock and sucking me into her mouth, making me forget my name, age, location. I focus on the intense pleasure she's giving me until the feeling winds up way too tight.

"Fuck," I curse, pulling out of her mouth. "I can't take it anymore," I say, admitting defeat. I want inside of her. Right fucking now.

"Good," she says with a smirk, wrapping her arms around my neck. "Neither can I." Her lips find mine as she kisses me, dragging me onto the bed, on top of her, while I reach around to take her bra off, until she's completely naked.

"Fuck me, Chris," she pleads, bumping her hips up so her pussy grazes my cock.

I look down at her, seeing her cheeks flushed, and her eyes burning with need. I spread her legs open with my knee, and grab my cock in my hand, fitting it against her entrance. I run my dick along her pussy, coating myself in her wetness before I slide inside, both of us moaning as soon as I do.

"Fuck," she gasps. "More."

I thrust deeper inside her, letting out a groan when I'm to the hilt. "Christ, Gabi. Fuck, you feel so good, baby," I murmur, sliding a few inches out before I thrust right back into her tight pussy. "You're gripping me so tight."

Her moans of pleasure make my balls wind up tight, and I lean down to kiss her, needing to be as close as physically possible. I'm inside of her body, her skin plastered against mine, her lips on mine and I still need closer.

"I love the noises you make," she says against my lips as moan after moan leaves mine. The pleasure I feel is un-fucking-describable, and I can't help the noises that leave me.

"I know," I reply with a grin. "Your pussy drips whenever I moan in your ear," I tease her, kissing her full pink lips. "So fucking wet. So tight."

"Chris," she yells out, her hands grabbing my ass to push me deeper inside of her, harder, faster.

"No one can hear you," I tell her, grabbing her hands and pinning them above her head, our fingers intertwining. "It's just us. Let it out, Gabi."

I thrust into her until Gabi shakes underneath me, her face screwing up tight as she comes, flooding my cock.

"Shit," I gasp, feeling her tighten around me. "I'm not going to last."

"I don't want you to," she says, breathlessly. "Come inside me," she says, her pussy fluttering around my cock. "Fill me with your cum."

Jesus. Her filthy fucking mouth gets me every time. My cock thrusts into her one, two more times until my balls tighten up and I come inside of her, continuing slow, lazy thrusts as I empty deep inside of her.

I fall to the bed once we've both come down from the high and immediately pull her into me, needing to kiss her, to feel her. "Fuck," I murmur against her lips. "I can't wait to do that with you for the rest of our lives."

She chuckles, reaching for my hand to intertwine our fingers together. "Hey, you have another one of my firsts."

My lips are parted as heavy breathes leave me, and I furrow my brows, wondering what the hell she's talking about.

She must see my confusion from my expression, because she rolls on top of me, her tits pressed against my chest and leans down to brush her lips against mine. "My first time having sex with my husband."

I let out a laugh, and cup her face, kissing her again. "Damn right. And I'll have all of your lasts, too, pretty girl."

Chapter 23

GABRIELLA

I'm officially a married woman.

Which means if Channing Tatum somehow finds me and falls desperately in love with me—as I know he would—I would have to turn him down. I wonder if that's the real reason Chris wanted to get married.

I didn't need to be married to be loyal. Even while being his girlfriend, I wouldn't leave him. Not even for Channing Tatum.

My husband is hot. Smoking fucking hot.

My smile widens as I watch him, lying on my stomach with my chin resting on my hands, propped up on my elbows. He's sprawled on his back—who the hell sleeps on their back? *Weirdo*—with his hand flat on his toned, bare stomach. I can't resist leaning over to flick my tongue against his cheek.

One eye snaps open, and he lets out a low chuckle, his morning raspy voice sending a shiver through me. "Did we get a dog, or did you just lick me?"

"It was just me," I confirm.

He laughs, opening his eyes fully before turning on his side to face me. He pulls me into him, our bodies plastered together. "Good morning, wife," he murmurs, kissing me lightly.

I arch a brow. "Is that my new nickname?"

His shoulders shake with a quiet laugh. "You know you'll always be my pretty girl," he says, with a smirk. "But I can't fucking help it. I love calling you my wife."

A needy noise leaves my lips when he kisses my neck, nuzzling his head into me. "I love hearing it," I tell him.

He hums against my skin, rolling me onto my back as he kisses my neck, my chest. Not one ounce of my skin goes untouched by him. "We're married," I murmur as he continues his slow kisses.

"I know," he says, lifting his head with an amused look in his eyes. "I was there."

My lips lift in a smile as I let my hands slide to his neck, gripping his hair between my fingers. "You're my husband," I say, trying out the words. I've only said it a couple of times, and it still sounds so weird, so new... but so right.

"And you're my wife," Chris says, kissing my arm before he lifts my hand and kisses right on my wedding band.

I can't help but think of how long I've known him. I practically grew up with him. My life was entangled with him, until we were ripped apart senior year of high school. I wonder what my life would have been like if I never met him. If he didn't come back to me.

"Did you think we'd be here?" I ask him, curious to know his answer. "When we met, sixteen years ago, did you think we'd be married?"

He arches a brow. "Seeing as I was twelve, probably not, but when we got older ..." He trails off, his eyes meeting mine. "I hoped for it," he says, making my heart ache. "I was obsessed with you. Crazy in love with you and you barely looked my way. Not how I wanted, anyway."

My frown is instant, remembering all the years I was oblivious to Chris's feelings for me. I wish I knew. I wish someone slapped me in the face and told me he was everything I wanted. It wasn't until our senior year of high school, that I started to develop feelings for him. And when I finally fell in love with him... everything turned to shit.

"I guess I just lost hope," he continues, his eyes tinged with a sad look. "As we grew up, and I saw you dating other people... I didn't think it would ever happen," he admits.

I can't even imagine a world where we're not together. I can't even begin to understand how I ever looked at him and didn't realize how much I loved him.

"I'm sorry I took so long," I tell him, feeling his soft hair between my fingers. "I'm sorry I didn't figure out my feelings for you sooner."

He shakes his head slightly, lifting my hand to his mouth as he kisses my wedding ring again. "I would have waited an eternity for you."

Fuck. My eyes start to tear up, and ugh. I blink back the tears, letting out a laugh. "You're being way too romantic," I tell him. "Fuck me. I'm horny."

Chris tips his head back with a laugh, shaking his head down at me. "You're insatiable."

"You should have known that before you married me," I tell him, rolling him onto his back so I can straddle him. "Now you're stuck with me," I tease, reaching down to grip his cock, which is already thick and hard in my fist. "You're hard?" I ask, arching a brow.

He chuckles. "You're here."

I stroke him slowly, loving his answer. "And that's all it takes?"

He nods, groaning when I start to stroke him a little harder, a little faster. "You look at me and my body aches for you."

I lean down to kiss him, smiling against his mouth and let my hand fall from his cock, shuffling on his lap so his cock fits between my pussy lips as I start to slowly rub myself on him.

"Christ, you're so fucking wet," he grunts, gripping my thighs as I continue to move my hips back and forth, the tip of his dick hitting my clit just right. "God, that's so… ugh." Chris thrusts his hips, cum shooting out of his cock a second later.

I keep moving my hips, moaning at the feel of his cock rubbing against my clit as I swipe my finger across his stomach, licking the cum off. "I wanted this inside me," I tell him with an arched brow.

He chuckles, groaning as I keep moving. "You want me to impregnant you already?" he teases.

I pause, placing my hands flat on his stomach as I stop moving, my brows furrowing as I look down at him. "That would be too crazy… right?" I ask, anticipating his response.

"I mean…" He shrugs. "Not really."

I blink. "No?"

He shrugs again. "We want a family someday, right?"

Hearing the word family makes my lips twitch into a smile. We both had a fucked-up family growing up, so the thought of us making our own little family heals a part of me that I didn't realize was still broken.

"We just got married," I point out.

He shakes his head. "I would have had a baby with you even before you had my ring on your finger," he says, tracing said ring with his thumb.

Something settles inside me. "You would?"

He nods, his eyes earnest. "I want everything with you," he says. "The thought of seeing your belly plump and round with my baby makes me really fucking happy." His eyes light up, and my heart races with the love I have for him.

I lean down to brush my lips against his. "I can't wait to have a family with you," I tell him.

He cups my face, returning my smile. "We can talk about all of the details later," he says. "Now get on my cock. I want inside you."

I let out a laugh, arching a brow. And he calls *me* insatiable. "Already?"

"I told you," he says with a smirk. "You look at me and I'm ready to go."

I lift onto my knees, wrap my fist around his cock and slowly lower onto him, inch by torturous inch, letting out a deep moan when I'm all the way to the hilt.

"Fuck," he groans when I lift off his cock, only to slam back down, the feel of him deep inside of me too much to handle. "That's it. Ride me." His low, husky voice brings out a moan deep from my throat as I place my hands flat on his chest, grinding my clit against his pelvis every time I drop onto his cock.

"God," I gasp, throwing my head back. "This feels so fucking good."

Chris lets out soft moans, his heavy breaths of pleasure making me wetter as he reaches up and toys with my nipple piercings, making the pleasure grow with each second.

"I'm almost there," I murmur, squeezing my eyes closed as the feeling crests. "Fuck. Yes. Yes. Y—"

I gasp when a knock hits our door, and I jump off Chris's cock, pulling the sheet up.

"*Oh no*," I hear Grayson's dry voice from the other side of the door. "Did I interrupt you guys?" My eyes narrow when I hear his low chuckle.

"Go the fuck away," I call out.

"This is revenge for cockblocking me this whole week," he says with another laugh.

I groan, burying my head in my hands. "I'm going to fucking kill him."

Chris lets out a laugh, pulling my hands away. "Good thing I'm your husband now," he says with a smirk. "I can't testify against you."

His soft brown eyes make me smile. "You'd kill him with me?" I tease.

Chris sputters out a cough. "Maybe let's put murder in the backburner for now," he jokes. "It's only one more day, baby," he says, rolling on top of me. "One more day, and then we're on our way to our honeymoon."

My smile widens. "And no more Grayson."

"And no more Grayson," he repeats with a laugh, leaning down to kiss me. When he pulls back, he grips my waist and flips me over, pressing down on my back to create the perfect arch. "Now, be a good girl and spread your legs. I'm not done with you yet."

Chapter 24

CHRISTOPHER

"No more," James says with a groan, dropping his head onto the table. "Please."

"One more," Grayson says, holding up another shot of tequila. "You doubled down on the bet, you have to live with the consequences."

James lets out an agonized noise as he rolls his head back, screwing his face when he looks at the shot in Grayson's hand. "God, I'm not young like I used to be."

"We're literally still in our twenties," Grayson replies, arching a brow. "Stop trying to make us sound old."

James squints. "You sure look it, grandpa."

He holds the shot up to James, narrowing his eyes at him. "Drink."

"Come on, gorgeous," Aiden says with a laugh as he tries to get Leila to stop checking her phone, which she has been doing since she got here. "Talia's fine. Both of our girls are."

Leila lets out a sigh. "I miss her."

"Me too," he replies, leaning down to press a kiss to her cheek. "But it's Gabi and Chris's last night with us, before they leave for their honeymoon. Let's enjoy the night off." He kisses her again, and she melts into him, her lips curving in a smile.

"When are you guys leaving anyway?" Leila asks.

"Early tomorrow morning," Gabi says, smiling as her eyes meet mine. "It's our last night in New York before we're off to Paris."

"And Spain," I add.

"And London," Gabi finishes. "Together this time."

I think of all the times I told her we'd get away together. And how much it hurt her when I did it without her. But now, we're going together, and I'm going to do it right this time. Visit all the places I wish we could have seen together.

"Sounds like an expensive trip," Grayson says with a snicker.

Gabi turns her gaze on me, her lips turning in a smirk. "Good thing my husband's rich."

I let out a laugh. "Did you marry me for my money?"

"Of course," she jokes. "I like pretty things."

I shake my head, leaning closer to her. "I don't even care," I admit with a smile. "I'll have you any way possible, as long as you're mine."

"I always have been," she replies, her eyes shining. "Since I was twelve."

"And I was always yours." I curl my hand over the back of her neck, and tug her toward me, bringing our lips together.

"Alright," James says an eye roll. "Save it for the honeymoon." Gabi chuckles at his expression. "Here," he says, sliding some drinks toward us. "Let's play a game, since you're all boring married couples now."

"You just don't want to be the only one who's drunk," Grayson adds with a laugh. "Besides, Rosie and I aren't even married yet."

"Come on," he says. "This is our final game together."

"Highly doubt that's true," I add.

"What game?" Lucas asks, his brows furrowed.

James smiles, knowing his best friend has his back and he grabs more drinks, placing them in front of us. "Two truths and one lie," he says. "Whoever gets the answer wrong, drinks."

"Fine by us," Aiden says with a chuckle as he wraps his arm around Leila's shoulder, since they don't drink.

"Cheaters," James murmurs, before he sits back down, beside his husband. "I'll go first." He clears his throat, tapping his chin, and then sits up straight. "I once threw a can at an old woman's head, I once wore my underwear for a week straight, and I like balls."

Grayson lets out a scoff. "Are any of them a lie?"

"It has to be the first one," Madeline says, blinking. "Right?"

Lucas laughs, shaking his head. "You'd be surprised, *princesa*."

Carter squints at his boyfriend, pursing his lips. "I don't even know this one."

Aiden slaps his hand against the table. "The second one," he says. "I'm calling it."

"Final answers?" James asks, drumming on the table as we nod. "It was the second one," he says, which makes a couple of people groan as they pink up their drink and take a sip. "I would never wear my underwear for more than a day, are you kidding?" he says, like he's actually offended. "I'm not Grayson."

Grayson narrows his eyes at him. "I've never once done that."

James scoffs. "Sure you haven't," he says, throwing him a wink, which makes Grayson shake his head in confusion.

"Wait a minute," I say. "You threw a can at an old lady?"

He scoffs, nodding. "Hell yes. This old bitch cut in line at the supermarket, and was rude as fuck. I had to put her in her place."

We all watch him, our mouth dropped open. "James," Lucas reprimands him, like he would a child.

"She was fine," he says with an eye roll. "The ambulance showed up right away."

The air is quiet as we all stare at him, until Aiden clears his throat. "Okay, moving on…" He straightens his back, tapping on the table. "I'll go next. I can recite the entire script of *High School Musical* from memory. I got into a fight with a bear, and I won a hot dog eating contest for eating fifty hot dogs in under five minutes."

"The last one," Grayson says. "For sure. There's no way you can finish that many hot dogs."

Gabi sputters out a cough. "Did you guys forget the second one? He wouldn't be able to survive."

"You never know," Grayson replies. "He has muscles and shit."

Leila scoffs. "They're not that big."

Aiden smirks down at her. "Just say you want to kiss me and stop flirting with me in front of our friends."

Leila rolls her eyes. "You wish."

"Pssst." Gabi whispers, getting Leila's attention. "You know the answer, don't you?"

Leila's lips twitch. "Might do."

Gabi's eyes widen. "What is it?" she asks. "Tell me and I'll give you my first born."

"I'm good," Leila replies, amused. "I've already got two children."

Gabi lets out a loud gasp that raises the attention of everyone at this bar, placing a hand on her chest, dramatically. "You're saying you don't want my child?"

Leila laughs with a shake of her head at Gabi's antics.

"It's definitely the bear," I pipe up.

"I second that," James says with a nod. "The bear."

"Fuck it." Grayson lets out a sigh. "I change my answer. I say the bear, too."

Aiden laughs, shaking his head. "You're all wrong."

"How the fuck?" Grayson narrows his eyes. "You did not fight a bear."

Aiden shrugs, a mischievous smirk on his lips. "I never said what kind of bear it was."

His eyes widen. "No."

"Yes," he agrees with another laugh. "It was Nova's teddy bear. She cried when she tripped over it, so I pretended to fight the bear to avenge my daughter's toe."

"No way in hell," Gabi says with narrowed eyes. "That's cheating."

"No," Aiden replies with a scoff. "It's just being smart. Drink up," he says, gesturing to our drinks.

James groans, shaking his head. "Not again. Please. I can't take another sip of alcohol."

Carter chuckles, reaching for James's drink and drinks it for him.

James's eyes zone in on his husband. "I love you," he murmurs, slightly slurring his words.

"You're drunk," his husband replies amused.

James just shrugs. "Still love you."

I take a sip of my drink, noticing how Gabi places her drink back down, looking as full as it was before. Huh. Weird. Maybe she just wants to be up early for the flight tomorrow, and not wake up with a headache. Whatever it is, I'm not about to call out my girl.

"My turn," Gabi says, clearing her throat, everyone's attention turning to her. She glances at the girls, her eyes getting teary as they nod. The fuck is going on? My brows furrow as I watch her take a deep breath. "I just got married, I have blue eyes," she starts, making me even more confused. Why the hell would she make these so obvious? Gabi loves to win a game.

She turns toward me, and holds my eyes as she says, "And I'm not pregnant."

My heart stops. Halts in my chest with every second her eyes are on me stretching to infinity.

"What?" I repeat, my ears ringing as the guys around me all celebrate.

She doesn't acknowledge them, keeping her eyes on me as her lips curve into a beautiful smile. "Surprise."

My eyes widen and I lift off my chair, gripping her waist in my hand and spin her around. "Holy shit," I yell, a huge grin breaking out on my face. "You're kidding," I say, hoping this isn't some sort of prank.

She laughs, tilting her head back when we finally come to a stop. "No," she confirms. "I'm serious."

Our eyes meet as I shake my head, unable to process it. "You're pregnant?"

She nods, tugging her bottom lip between her teeth as she wraps her arms around my neck, leaning closer to me. "Are you excited?" she asks. "I know it's a little earlier than we had planned but—"

I kiss her. I lean down and kiss her because I'll burst if I don't. "Of course I'm excited. Oh my god." I glance down at her flat stomach. Realistically I know it's probably too early to see anything, but just the thought of our child being inside her makes me feel dizzy. A wedding and a baby all in one weekend. I'm going to die of happiness.

"We're going to have a baby?" I ask her again, trying to get my mind to catch up.

"We're going to have a baby," she repeats with a laugh. "I told the girls before the wedding," she admits. "I was so nervous about your reaction."

I arch a brow. "Is that why you asked me all those questions yesterday?"

She nods. "I was scared you'd tell me you didn't want kids," she admits, her voice a little quieter. "I know our childhood was hard and we both had shitty dads but—"

"We won't be like that," I promise her, holding her face in my hands. "We're going to be amazing parents, Gabi. We're going to give our children everything we never had. We're going to make them feel loved, and nurtured and cherished." She melts into my hands, her eyes fluttering closed. "We're going to be a family."

She opens her eyes, a smile spreading across her face. "We're going to be a family," she repeats, testing out the words on her tongue.

I nod, staring at my best friend, the love of my life, and mother of my child. "I can't wait to start our life together."

"Forever," she says.

"Until the day I stop breathing," I promise her, secretly thanking every star that brought us together.

THE END

Family Tree

Rosalie Grace Livingston

Grayson Carter Livingston

Daniel Gary Livingston

Leila Juliana Pierce

Aiden Matthew Pierce

Nova Valeria Pierce

Talia Camila Pierce

Asher Cameron Pierce

Madeline Amara Silva

Lucas Rafael Silva

Malik James Silva

Ciara Nia Silva

Gabriella Hudson

Christopher Hudson

Millie Hope Hudson

Dylan Elio Hudson

Acknowledgements

We have finally made it to the end of the Campus Games Series. I still can't believe this is the end.

When I first started writing this series, I was unemployed and just writing for fun, wanting to write my own stories for the first time. I never thought I would be here two years later with the final installment of the Campus Games series and amazing followers and readers.

I am so thankful for you guys and for everyone who has read or shared my book. Without you, I wouldn't be here, and this series wouldn't be written.

These characters mean so much to me and I had the best time writing their books. I am so happy that you guys have found solace in these characters and their stories and that you have related to them as I have.

Thank you for joining my author journey through this series, and I hope you continue to stick with me with the next upcoming books.

.

About the Author

Stephanie Alves is an avid reader and writer of smutty, contemporary romance books. She was born in England, but was raised by her loud Portuguese parents. She can speak both languages fluently, though she tends to mix both languages when speaking. She loves to write romantic comedies with happy endings, witty banter and sizzling chemistry that will make you blush. When she's not writing, she can be found either reading, or watching rom coms with her two adorable dogs cuddled up beside her.

You can find her here:
Instagram.com/Stephanie.alves_author
Stephaniealvesauthor.com

Printed in Great Britain
by Amazon